KINDLY LIGHT

'We shall never be able to park here, sir,' said the chauffeur.

'Drop us on the corner of Berwick Street, Rowell. We can easily walk from there.'

The car pulled up by a shop called LOVEMAKING which appeared, from the wares advertised in the window, to sell moulds for making candles. Sir Alfred pointed it out to the two priests in passing with a despondent shrug, and led them off with the air of one who knew every inch of the streets they were traversing.

In spite of the frosty weather, there were lots of people about. Young men that Norman's father would have called dagoes lolled in every doorway, their street cries advertising a range of diversions, literary, cinematographic and sensual.

'Hey, sir, you like a very nice, very young virgin?'

'Take no notice, Shotty,' said Sir Alfred.

'How much?' Norman asked.

A.N. Wilson

KINDLY LIGHT

ARROW

Arrow Books Limited
17–21 Conway Street, London W1P 6JD

An imprint of the Hutchinson Publishing Group

London Melbourne Sydney Auckland
Johannesburg and agencies throughout
the world

First published in Great Britain by
Martin Secker & Warburg Ltd 1979
Hamlyn Paperbacks edition 1983

Arrow edition 1985

© A.N. Wilson 1979

Printed and bound in Great Britain by
Hazell Watson & Viney Limited,
Aylesbury, Bucks

ISBN 0 09 940550 4

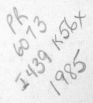

All the characters and institutions in this story are imaginary, including those of the Archbishop and the British Consul in Jerusalem.

1

The Encircling Gloom

The women who danced round the table wore only black fish-net stockings and the briefest of gym-tunics. They were singing a medley of Beatles hits.

ALL YOU NEED IS LOVE. ALL YOU NEED IS LOVE.

They did not conform to Norman Shotover's idea of what nuns ought to be like. Nor did he agree with the message of their lyric. If he had done, he would never have joined the Roman Church; still less, committed himself to membership of one of its strictest orders, the Catholic Institute of Alfonso.

I MAY NOT HAVE A LOT TO GIVE, BUT WHAT I GOT I GIVE TO YOU.

Some of the nuns looked terrible. It had been a big mistake to give up wearing the habit. In the old days, they had all looked the same. Now, one was made aware of wobbling thighs, hairy armpits, varicose veins bulging their way through nylon.

The Father Provincial had drawn the line at having the nuns in the Chapel, and so Mass was being held in the recreation room. But it had been his idea, for the Christmas retreat, to have something modern. Word had got back to the Institute that people considered the order, its comfortable mother house, its fitted carpets, its fashionable Mayfair church, its list of distinguished but old-fashioned converts, as 'stick in the mud'. For Norman Shotover, of course, who had been looking all his life for some mud to be stuck into, it seemed ideal. But the Father Provincial was a man of broader vision. Correspondents to the *Tablet* and other religious periodicals, who have more zest for ugly clichés than do most of the human race, asked from time to time when the

7

Institute of Alfonso was going to be dragged 'kicking and screaming into the twentieth century'. Father Cassidy would show them that kicking and screaming would be unnecessary. They would do it dancing. For this purpose, he had enlisted the help of Adrian Sporran and his order of dancing nuns, all the rage nowadays in charismatic circles. They had motored in to conduct the retreat from the Pentecost Centre, their convent in Luton.

The singing had stopped now. The Reverend Mother had put down her guitar on the Holy Table, and Father Sporran had begun to read the Gospel. He had a distinguished voice, fundamentally aristocratic, with touches of army. The sound seemed to be coming from the back of his throat but it was as if, for the best egalitarian reasons, his tongue was trying to smother it on the way out . . . In anyone less modern, one would have thought the voice 'plummy'.

'Once a guy gave a party and asked a crowd of friends; and he sent his liaison officer to tell them when the nosh was up. But they all tried to split. One said. "I can't come because I'm a big property speculator and I've been corrupted by my possession of capital." Another said, "There's this hassle over my factory farm, so I can't come." Another said, "I have a marital problem, so I can't come either." And when the officer liaised with the guy about the situation he was mad, and said, "Go out into the underprivileged parts of this urban area, and bring in the lower-paid income bracket, the visually handicapped and the disabled . . . " '

Most of Norman's fellow-priests looked as bewildered as he did by this recitation; except Lubbock of course, who was entering into the spirit of the 'retreat' with a maddening degree of enthusiasm.

But there was worse to come. When the Gospel was over, Father Sporran sat down and asked if they would like to have a short discussion of its implications. Lubbock needed very little prompting.

Lubbock's 'accent' – if that is not too strong a word for the very faint deviations from the normal which characterized his speech – was difficult to place. It certainly did deviate, but the sound had no obvious provenance. The messages it seemed to give out were more of mood than of region; an indication to its hearers, if they could have been in any doubt of the fact, that Lubbock was in some manner hard done by. It was distinctive enough to lend credibility to his assertions that he had 'come up the hard way', suffered difficulties in early life greater than most people's; been cruelly maltreated and misunderstood by the world. At the same time, it was quite mild enough to be discarded without giving the impression of affectation when a more exuberant mood overtook him. Then exotic origins could be hinted at, influential friends, even a suggestion, imitated from the Provincial's conversational manner, that he knew what was going on behind the scenes in the high places of the world. But at no stage could his voice ever be thought melodious or pleasing to the ear. It had a perpetually rasping note which made his utterances, even when good-humoured or witty, which they could be, approximate to a sneer, and which moved uneasily between crowing and whining. Moreover, he *burbled*, so that it was only when he was in mid-sentence that one became aware that he had started to talk. 'And anyway,' he was saying, 'why couldn't the cattle-farmer come to the party? Probably too busy at milking time.'

There was a short pause, while everyone waited to see if the point was going to be developed. Lubbock's mind had a way of going off at a tangent, so that it was never possible to be sure whether he was talking nonsense, or if he was on the verge of saying something startling and clever. The burbling had started again.

' . . . probably in a town. The party was probably in a town. Now, if it was in a town . . . It all anticipates . . . you see, the Industrial Revolution. It's like Blake . . . '

Father Sporran looked displeased by this interruption. Lubbock had expressed great enthusiasm for the charismatic movement at every stage of the retreat, without showing in the slightest degree that he knew what it was. It was possible that he was going to have to be called to order.

Father Sporran was good at calling people to order. Those

who knew him well said that he was the bossiest man in the world, and Norman could have believed it had he not met the Provincial. Father Sporran had been a Guards officer before being ordained, and the opportunity for giving people directions was clearly what had attracted him to priesthood in the Roman Church.

'Has anyone anything further to say about the Gospel?' he said. It was surprising, given the distaste he had for anyone's opinions other than his own, that he was insisting on the discussion at all. But he did not do things by halves. When reform had swept over the church, he was determined to be seen in the vanguard. Since 1963, he had been in love with all things modern, liturgically speaking at least. He felt the same should be demanded of his congregations, and he made it clear that he thought the present company gathered round the table were making a poor job of things, not pulling their weight. One of the nuns came to the rescue.

'I think that what Jesus is saying is that the Mass is just one big party where we can all enjoy ourselves,' she said gaily.

Lubbock, however, was still talking. He did not seem to notice that any other contributions had been made to the 'discussion'. ' . . . some of my ancestors were cattle rustlers in Berwickshire until the early years of the eighteenth century,' he said, changing gear into his 'grand' voice. No occasion was inappropriate, as far as he was concerned, for giving improbable accounts of his family history. 'As a matter of fact, *Lubbock* means *Rustler* in Dutch.'

Father Sporran conceded defeat, and briskly moved into the Offertory. He laid a scarlet serviette into a basket in front of him, on to which he placed a few slices of Hovis. Then he filled two large studio pottery mugs with Sainsbury's Beaujolais. Before long, Norman and the other priests were stretching out their arms over the little table to consecrate the bread and the wine.

In a troubling way, Norman had ceased to believe in it all. At the Anglo-Catholic church where he had first heard mass, it was surrounded by such an exotic aura of mystery and beauty that it was possible to believe, at the moment of elevation, when bells rang, and clouds of incense wafted round the altar, that God Himself had come down into the sacred elements. Without such theatrical aids to the imagination, it seemed a good deal less probable. He mumbled his way through the words with no feeling of awe, or interest. There were no genuflexions; not so much as a bow. The Hovis was not even lifted up; but, at the actual moment of the consecration, the nuns sang, 'Oh, yeah, Lord!'

The kissing came next. Norman had placed himself in the middle of the row of priests, near the Provincial, so there was no danger of his having to 'take' the kiss of peace to any of the nuns. Even so, this part of the rite embarrassed him. The American priest on his left shook his hand and said, 'God be with you, Norman.'

'Good afternoon,' he replied.

It was like that parlour game where you have to whisper a message in someone's ear, and they in turn have to pass it on to their neighbours. Norman turned to the Provincial, Father Cassidy, on his right.

He was a little afraid of the Provincial. Tiny eyes set behind thick spectacles seemed to peer telepathically into one's secret thoughts.

'Peace be with you, Father.'

'And also with you, my son.'

Painless. Soon over. Cassidy was as hard as nails. Embracing him was almost as agreeable as embracing no one at all. He doubtless had his reasons for allowing all these liturgical japes to disturb the week before Christmas. What they were, who could guess? Any distaste he might have felt for the charismatic Mass was certainly not allowed to show. His pudgy, slightly yellow face gave nothing away.

The kiss of peace went on down the line until it reached Lubbock. It was an obvious opportunity for the man to call attention to himself, and Norman wondered how he was going to do it. Everything about Lubbock had come to irritate Norman: his lean, beaky face, his darting eyes; his habit of swaying to and fro on his heels; his burbling. Since he was the last priest to receive the kiss of peace, it meant that

11

all attention focused on him. He smiled his inane, self-pitying smile, and advanced on the Reverend Mother.

She was a big woman to be wearing as little as a gym tunic, and sweat was pouring from her brow.

'Peace and love, Teresa.'

The very liquid quality of Lubbock's kiss was embarrassingly audible. Mother Teresa was too ecstatic to make any coherent reply, but one heard, 'Oh, Father!' gasped in tones of almost obscene abandon.

After that, the liturgy proceeded in more or less the normal way. Father Sporran distributed the Hovis, and Mother Teresa the wine. Then they sat down for a period of silent meditation. Father Cassidy told his beads during this interval, and stared at the floor.

For Norman, the sitting seemed to be interminable. Gradually, a curious high-pitched humming noise broke the silence. And then he realized that the nuns were about to burst into song once more.

'We shall overcome, we shall overcome, we shall overcome some day.'

Father Cassidy had stopped telling his beads and was looking up. A peculiar look of satisfaction had passed over his face. It was inconceivable that he was *moved* by the singing (as Norman, much against his better judgment, now was). The smile suggested that everything was under control. It was if some private joke had occurred to him, known only to himself and the Almighty.

The celebrant rose, and everyone else stood up. After a short prayer, he extended his hands and sang:

'The Mass is over now – go home!'

To which the nuns chanted the response:

'O–kaaaaaaaaaaaay!'

'You ought to be more open, more loving.'

'I know, Father. But I don't know how to be.'

'Just open your heart in prayer. You ought to learn to relax. Do you do Yoga?'

'No.'

'Try it. Now then, is there anything else?'

'I am absolutely obsessed by one of the priests here.'

'Physically obsessed?'

'Of course not.'

'But you are in love with him?'

'Quite the reverse. Everthing about him annoys me. He smells, he is attractive to women. He is totally unreliable. He never turns up for appointments. Everyone thinks highly of him. He is an egotist and a fraud. I *hate* him.'

'You must not give way to these feelings of irritation. They are very normal in communities like this. I remember having them in the army. How long have you been a member of the Institute?'

'Three years.'

'And you are a priest already?'

'I was a priest before I joined.'

'Ah, yes. I remember hearing about you. Well, sit lightly to your feelings of irritation. They are very close to feelings of love, you know.'

'Are they?'

'Yes, they are. Now, is there anything else?'

'I don't really believe in God any more.'

There was an agonizing silence. Norman peered through the grille to see if Father Sporran was still there. He was. It looked as if he had covered his face with his hands.

'How long has this been the case?' he asked eventually.

'I don't know. Ages.'

'None of us believe in God all the time. Faith means holding on in the dark when we don't feel anything, don't know anything. God tries us in that way. You are stuck in a groove here. You don't have enough experience of the world to be able to believe in God all the time. Have you ever thought of going to South America?'

'No.'

'They are crying out for priests in the shanty-towns. Think about it. For your penance, since you seem to like the old prayers, say the *Anima Christi* . . . Go in peace, and pray for me, a sinner.'

13

The retreat was over. Father Sporran and his dancing nuns had bundled their guitars into the back of a Dormobile and left for the suburbs after luncheon.

Norman had decided to devote the afternoon to Christmas shopping and pay his annual visit to Asprey, to buy a present for his father. But, just as he was on his way out of the house, he met the Provincial. He had been meaning to tell Father Cassidy for weeks that he wanted to leave the Institute. He assumed that it would be easy enough. Everyone was doing it nowadays. And he had promised himself that he would speak to Cassidy about it before Christmas.

'Ah, Norman.'

'Good afternoon, Father.'

'Just the man I was looking for.'

'Really? I wanted to speak to *you*.'

'No time for that, I'm afraid. Drop into my room some time after six o'clock. I've got to go out before the bank closes.'

On anyone else's lips, this announcement would have seemed ordinary enough; but Father Cassidy spoke in a cryptic manner which almost suggested that he was off to Threadneedle Street to prevent the final collapse of Sterling.

'It's something rather important,' said Norman.

'After six.' The reply was firm. 'What I wanted to see *you* about was this. Father Lubbock is looking for volunteers to decorate the refectory. I said you'd oblige. Run along now, like a good fellow.'

He was gone before there was any time to reply.

Norman was under obedience to Father Cassidy, so there was no way in which he could get out of it. Even if he had not been, he could hardly have refused. Father Cassidy had an authority of manner which was difficult to question. But there could scarcely be a drearier way of spending this first afternoon of freedom after the retreat than watching Lubbock hang up Christmas decorations. It was unfair. Norman had been asked to do it every year since he joined the Institute.

Lubbock was unpacking paper balls, tinsel, paper chains

14

and plastic holly from large cardboard containers when Norman reached the refectory.

'Shotty. Hallo there. Don't worry, you're not late.'

Norman hated this tedious abbreviation of his surname by which Lubbock chose to address him. And he thought Lubbock was a fine person to be commenting on his promptness or lack of it.

'I knew you'd enjoy this, Shotty. Just your cup of tea. Between ourselves, Father Cassidy wanted two of the Americans to help me. They had been asking for weeks if they could do it, but I knew you would be disappointed if you couldn't put up the decorations. You've done it every year since you came.'

'I'm perfectly happy for the Americans to do it. As a matter of fact, I should prefer it. I was just going out.'

'I wouldn't hear of it, Shotty, old thing. Just you start putting up a few streamers. I shall be back in a minute.'

He was gone again, almost at once.

Norman gazed at the tasteless decorations with misery. The sooner they were up, he supposed, the sooner he could go out. He decided not to waste any time hanging around for Lubbock.

Putting up the paper chains on his own was a tedious operation, involving the inevitable sense that step-ladders, drawing-pins and crêpe paper have a semi-animate ability to make the job more difficult than it need be. Indeed, by the time he was pinning the last end of the paper in a high corner of the room, Norman felt sweaty and cross. There was still no sign of Lubbock. His thumbs were sore with pushing in pins. It was all taking much longer than expected.

Yet he could not help feeling rather pleased with his efforts. Standing on a chair, he began to hang paper balls in the windows. All that remained was to put some plastic holly over the portraits of Cardinal Wiseman and Mary Queen of Scots, and he would still have time to walk down to Bond Street before the shops closed.

It was at this point that Lubbock returned, muttering something about a pain in his insides.

'Your ulcer again, I suppose?' Norman did *try* to be charitable.

'It's something worse, I think. I don't want to bore you with it.'

This was manifestly the reverse of the truth, but Norman did not say so.

'Do you think all those streamers look all right, meeting in the middle of the room like that, Shotty old thing?'

'Yes,' said Norman.

'They aren't all on one pin, are they?'

'No.'

Lubbock stood on a chair and stretched up towards them.

'I just wondered whether they are very secure,' he said. 'That's all. There! You see!'

The paper chains collapsed, swathing his neck and shoulders, giving him, for the moment, the appearance of some Fijian bridegroom decked in garlands.

'I thought so,' he said. 'Perhaps we should try putting them round the walls instead.'

'They were perfectly all right until you pulled at them.'

'But they weren't secure.'

It took hours to get the decorations just as Lubbock liked them. He kept imagining that one loop or another was asymmetrical, and that meant undoing them all and starting again. Then he altered the arrangement of paper balls in the windows. Finally, the plastic holly started to jump out from the portraits quite of its own accord.

Norman was too angry to speak. He felt overcome by hot, blinding irritation of an intensity not experienced since he had left school. He had reached the point where even to see Lubbock was a temptation to violence; but this was the last straw.

He could not remember if it had always been like this. Among Lubbock's many infuriating characteristics was the ability to make one feel ashamed of one's anger. He was, in many ways, an amiable man. He had intelligence of a sort. His combination of total egotism with apparent self-deprecation always hovered on the edge of being beguiling.

Just as one was feeling sorry for Lubbock, however, one would find oneself being put in one's place. Attention, not patronage, was what he craved, and he never responded with any enthusiasm to offers of 'help'.

His ulcer for instance. It so happened that Norman knew about ulcers. His father suffered from them, and on the rare occasions when they met in London, he would not infrequently allude to the fact. They saw each other more often than they once did. Colonel Shotover thought Catholicism was 'a lot of rot', as he had often pointed out. But at least joining an order had been one way out of the problem of what to do with Norman. There was less danger than ever of his wanting to come and stay.

'Just on my way to see old Grimblethorpe,' the Colonel would sometimes say, while toying with his lunch.

'In Harley Street?'

'Yup. I think it's this oast-house I've been living in. Have you seen it?'

'No. You've only been there six weeks.'

'It must have rising damp, or something. My stomach hasn't been right since I've been there. I'm looking round for something a bit more suitable.'

Norman could not remember a time when 'something a bit more suitable' was not being sought. He strolled with his father as far as Wigmore Street, where they parted.

'Look after yourself,' said the Colonel absently, and, having kissed Norman on both cheeks, was lost in the crowds.

When he turned round, Norman saw Lubbock standing a few yards away looking at a shop window. This ubiquity was another of his less endearing characteristics.

'Hallo,' he said, self-pityingly.

'Lubbock. What are you doing?'

'Trying to kill the pain.'

'Shouldn't you be in bed?'

'I've tried that. It just makes me sick.' He held on to his stomach melodramatically, as if vomiting might take place at any minute.

In fact, he looked in the pink. Apart from a rather doggy

17

look about the eyes, one would not have known there was anything wrong with him.

'Why not see a specialist?' Norman asked.

'Who, me?'

He gestured, as if such a worm as himself could not hope to claim the attentions of any member of the medical profession, still less a specialist.

'It would be sensible to get someone to look at you,' said Norman.

'But who?' Lubbock looked imploringly at him.

'My father's just gone to see a quack called Grimblethorpe. Said to be something of an expert on the internal organs. My father swears by him.'

'Your father?'

'I've just been seeing him for lunch.'

Lubbock always looked as if people were talking double-Dutch if they referred to activities not directly involving himself.

'You know so many people,' he said in a feeble tone of voice.

'Why not sign on? Grimblethorpe has a very good reputation.'

'Perhaps you could arrange it for me? I'd feel shy going to a grand place like that. You seem to forget that I didn't have a public school education.'

'What's that got to do with it?'

Lubbock merely sighed.

In other moods, when he was buoyant and more full of himself, Lubbock gave quite different accounts of his origins. There was vague talk of Harrow and quarrels with a sadistic housemaster. When the 'ulcer' was afflicting him, however, he liked to give the impression that he had endured great suffering in early life of a more plebeian order.

Norman accordingly rang up Grimblethorpe the next day and made an appointment for Lubbock to see him. He felt rather pleased with himself. He was aware that his dislike of Lubbock was unworthy and unwarranted, and these little acts of kindness helped to compensate for it. He reminded

Lubbock several times of the date of the appointment and even offered to go with him in a taxi.

'I can look after myself, thanks very much,' said Lubbock huffily. 'I'm not a child, you know.'

By the time the day came when Lubbock should have been seeing the specialist, his whole demeanour and physical appearance had changed. He was his old cocky self, boasting of how much work he was taking on, and how well he felt.

When evening came, Norman felt fairly sure that he would have cut the appointment with the doctor. He was merely interested to see how Lubbock justified himself.

'What did Grimblethorpe think about the ulcer?' he asked when he met Lubbock in the corridor on the way to supper.

'Grimblethorpe? What ulcer?'

'I thought you were seeing the specialist about your ulcer today.'

'You must have been thinking of someone else,' said Lubbock in accusing tones. He seemed to imply that one had no right to be thinking of anyone but himself. 'I'm much too ordinary to go round seeing grand people like specialists. The poor old National Health for the likes of me.'

The ability to behave as if he had no memory evidently served Lubbock's own baffling purposes well enough. At times, however, Norman wondered whether Lubbock was not losing his grip. He had a habit of repeating himself, which would have seemed loopy in a man twice his age. But one could not tell whether or not he knew he was doing it. Among the many energies which seemed to motivate him, guile was never absent.

Norman was astonished by the degree to which the rest of the Community seemed to accept Lubbock on his own very self-contradictory terms. If he said he was ill, they believed he was ill. When he claimed to be doing important work for the church, they appeared to believe that too. In fact, he seemed to do very little except moon about boasting or feeling sorry for himself. He claimed to be much in demand as a confessor. But, on several occasions, when Norman had been in the church hearing confessions himself, he had seen a

19

trickle of people waiting by Lubbock's confessional, and eventually going away again because he had forgotten to turn up. He would come into supper after evenings such as this, claiming that his penitents were wearing him out with the frequencey and diligence with which they desired his counsel.

All this seemed tantamount, in Norman's very limited experience of the world, to being mad; at the very least, faintly 'touched'. He could not see what other explanation there could be for such oddity of behaviour. He thought that the other priests, Father Cassidy in particular, should do something about it. But when he hinted as much to anyone else, they looked at him as if it was he, and not Lubbock, who was suffering from some psychological disorder.

He had come to the conclusion that the explanation for it all lay in Lubbock's possession of *charm*, a magical quality in which he knew himself to be lacking. People were always prepared to see Lubbock's absurdities in the light of deliberate clowning; his grovelling self-pity as humility; his boastfulness as high spirits; his reputed capacity for hard work as quite genuine; his apparent inactivity as evidence of a kind of *sprezzatura*, a wearing lightly of anything he undertook. He was a great 'character'. And that, apparently, justified anything.

Norman could see, not without traces of envy, that there was a sort of plausibility about Lubbock. When on form, he could be quite witty. He had a quickness of mind, even, on occasions, an ability to be funny about himself, which approached an admirable self-mockery. When his moods took an opposite turn, he had a power of convincing one that his troubles were of a truly monumental order: that his unhappiness was, in some way, deeper and more wretched than the common lot; and that his physical health was so fragile that he might at any moment collapse completely. Now, however, as he walked about the refectory putting the finishing touches to the Christmas decorations, Lubbock looked maddeningly agile and alive.

'What's the time?' asked Norman, hoping that the refectory clock was wrong, and that there was still time to go shopping.

'How should I know?' said Lubbock.

He had wasted the whole of Norman's afternoon. As well as the shopping, he had hoped to devote some time to clarifying the reasons he was going to give Father Cassidy for wanting to leave the order. It was too late to leave now before Christmas. But he intended to be out before much of the new year was past. This afternoon with Lubbock almost made him wonder whether he should not simply walk out of the front door and leave them all behind without saying a word.

'Well, that's enough of my valuable time devoted to frivolities. I hope you enjoyed yourself, Shotty old thing. I know how you like Christmas.'

'Goodbye, Lubbock.'

'What?'

'I'm going upstairs.'

'So am I. I'll come up with you.'

Father Cassidy sat in his study listening to the six o'clock news. There had been another run on the pound; the Government of Italy had fallen; riots were reported in a remote province of China. Cassidy nodded at the predictability of it all. How far his sense of personal responsibility for these, and most other things which took place in the world, was justified, it was impossible to know. Fantasy was kept so rigidly in check in his life that megalomania was never allowed to show.

The English Province of the Catholic Institute of Alfonso was not a large one. But it was not without influence. Since the order was founded in the sixteenth century, ostensibly for the suppression of heresy, it had been interfering in the internal affairs of almost every country in the world. There had never been an Englishman chosen as the General of the order before. But Father Cassidy liked to believe that there was a first time for everything. The General of the Institute was a powerful man; more powerful, some said, than the Pope himself.

When the weather, for which Father Cassidy felt no more than partially responsible, followed the news, he switched off his wireless and sat down at his writing-table. Selecting a magazine from the pile there, he opened it at page one, and laboriously began his perusal of its contents. It only had a few photographs, most of them of women in rubber diving suits. It was the twelfth publication of the kind that he had read that day. There had been one full of large bosomy women dressed in mortar-boards and wielding canes; another with pictures of lesbians dressed as firemen and brandishing hosepipes; now this.

Father Cassidy looked at his watch. He snorted. He would read one more before saying his office. His pallid, fat face was totally expressionless as it stared at the page in front of him, an account of why a young man liked wearing rubber under-pants. It made dull reading, and only increased the faint contempt in which Father Cassidy held the human race. There were so many other pleasures in life: gambling, intrigue, fishing. He could not understand why people wasted their money on this sort of thing.

There was a knock at the door.

'Come in.'

Norman Shotover entered, with a cautious air which suggested that he had come into the room by mistake.

'Ah, Norman.'

The Provincial blinked at his visitor. He knew that it was not going to be an easy interview. He had had his own reasons for allowing Norman to join the Institute some years before, but the young man had not settled to the life at all well. He was touchy and difficult with his fellow-priests, without any apparent compensatory deviousness or ingenuity.

Having been illegally ordained by a wandering bishop of the Eastern church, Norman had joined the Church of England, got himself tangled up with a lot of girls and finally jumped off the tower of a cathedral with a hang glider. Father Cassidy knew that it was all a good deal less casual than it sounded. Nor could he believe that it was mere chance that made Norman land in the garden of the Institute's retreat house in Sussex. The Provincial had been there himself when it happened. One of the more superstitious lay-brothers had thought it was the Second Coming, a young man drifting on wings through the sky. He had soon changed his mind when Norman had come to live in the house.

Father Cassidy still felt it was right to have admitted Norman. He had theories about him. No one in reality could be so dilatory, so childish, so ignorant of the ways of the world. The more Norman persisted in giving the appearance of possessing these qualities, the more Father Cassidy became convinced that they were not real. His very arrival, hurtling through the sky like Icarus, should have put everyone on the alert. Most of the other priests treated Norman as an amiable innocent; Father Cassidy saw no reason why he should not pretend to do the same.

The Provincial smiled impenetrably at Norman.

'I'm sorry to be a little late,' said Norman.

He appeared to be obsessed by punctuality.

'Lubbock and I were putting up paper chains, but he did not turn up for a long time. Then they all fell down . . . '

Father Cassidy disliked Norman's venomous inability to get along with Lubbock, a most valued member of the community. He dismissed it peremptorily.

'Lubbock is a sick man, and a busy man. Much in demand. You're not late. I was just about to say Vespers. Now you're here, we can say it together.'

'Of course.'

Norman knelt down and made the sign of the cross.

'Not now. Not just yet. We must have a little talk first.'

Norman sat down on the hard chair opposite the writing-table. His eye fell on the magazines which littered its surface. He wondered what the Provincial was doing with so many of them, and why he had not hidden them away when he heard a knock at the door.

'Have you enjoyed the retreat, Norman?'

'It was a bit noisy.'

'Father Sporran is a good man – a saint, some say. Not everyone likes his modern ways. I don't myself. Those nuns

23

are out of control. And I'm not sure about all this dancing at Mass. It destroys the old spirit of devotion. There's no doubt at all about that.'

'I thought retreats were meant to be quiet.'

'So they are. Father Sporran and his nuns have different ideas, you see. We have to move with the times. But he is a very disciplined man. He knows a lot about prayer, a lot about the spiritual life. I respect that, and so should you. He's a very experienced confessor. I suggested to you that you use the retreat as an opportunity for thinking about your future.'

'Yes, Father.'

'And did you do that?'

'Not really, Father.'

'Did you talk to Father Sporran about it?'

'He seemed to think I ought to go and work in shanty-towns in South America.'

'Did he now?'

Father Cassidy was silent for a while. He doodled on his blotter the words 'COFFEE – URANIUM?' and then scratched them out before speaking again.

'South America, was it? Well, if that is what God is calling you to do, that is what you will have to do. We've all got to have a social conscience nowadays, you know. And you know why?'

'No.'

'Because the Holy Father says that we must, and what he says still goes, in spite of the Council. Mind you, there are ways and ways of having a social conscience. Look at this for example.'

He held up a picture of a Negress being given the cane by someone dressed as postman. Norman peered, hoping that the social message would become plain. Perhaps the lady owned a ferocious dog which had bitten the man in uniform, or could it be some rather unpleasant propaganda from the National Front?

'What is it?' he asked.

'Can you not see for yourself?'

24

'I mean, why are you reading it?'

'It's filth,' said Father Cassidy. 'It's all part of this campaign by Sir Alfred Toogood to stamp out filth. You must have heard of it?'

'Yes.'

'He's one of the most pious Catholics in the House of Commons; and a Labour Party man. That's where your social conscience comes in. He has set up a committee to look into some of the vicious nonsense like this that is going on. I'm on the committee.' He added this late detail as if it went without saying.

'What can the committee do?' Norman asked.

'Well, we can keep abreast of what's being published. I'm mostly concentrating on the sado-masochistic stuff myself. That and rubber fetishism. Another member of the committee is doing paederasts, and so on. Then, tonight, some of us are going to a night-club. A real live show. It goes on till three o'clock in the morning. And to think what a busy day I have tomorrow. I shall have to be up early to say mass for some nuns. After that, there is another meeting with the Cardinal to discuss the Safe Period. And, in the afternoon, I have promised to give Benediction to a parish and start the Bingo. They're raising money for their pilgrimage to Lourdes. Ah dear, how the work of holy Church goes on.'

'It certainly seems to.'

'Father Sporran thinks you should go to South America, does he?'

'It was just an idea.'

'And what do you think?'

Norman blushed and looked at the floor. He had never greatly warmed to Father Cassidy, but the man had, in a funny sort of way, been kind to him. Although he could now see that joining the order had been a colossal error of judgment, they had fed him, clothed him and housed him for three years. In return, he had done almost nothing, except say mass, and prepare a few children for confirmation. These things were not to be underestimated. It was not the Institute's fault – or not entirely – that he now felt as he did.

'Father . . . I . . . '

'Yes?'

'What I wanted to talk to you about was . . . '

'Yes?'

'My future.'

'Good.'

'It's not that easy.'

'No. Well, you were an unusual case, Norman. You needed a couple of years after joining the Institute to find your feet. I'm glad you can see the future more clearly. It is something to thank God for.'

'I want to leave,' Norman blurted out.

'Are you feeling sick?'

'I mean, I want to leave the order. I want to give up being a priest. I want to give up being a Catholic.'

Father Cassidy allowed himself a faint smirk at this piece of rhetoric.

'Would it help you to say why?'

Norman crossed his legs and examined his finger-nails. He knew that Father Cassidy was capable of talking anyone out of any opinion, however firmly entrenched; and he had told himself, before coming into the room, that nothing, however persuasive, would make him change his mind.

'It was a mistake in the first place. I never meant to become a priest. I don't believe in God. I'm not happy.'

He was doing badly. Father Cassidy was smiling at the inadequacy of his line of reasoning.

'There's so much of the work of the Church that you haven't tried,' he said. 'Marriage guidance, for example. Then there is the question of homosexuality being opened up for the first time in the church's history. There is sex education in schools . . . '

'Doesn't the Catholic Church think about anything else except sex?'

'That and money. We tried you on an accountancy course, and the Bursar thought that you had no aptitude for it. There's a lot of important work to be done with stocks and shares, God knows. But we need men who are good at it; men

26

who can play the market.'

'I see.'

'If you really feel incapable of doing anything useful, we can arrange for you to write a thesis at Martyr Hall in Cambridge. But that's usually a last-ditch measure. I wouldn't be happy about your doing that.'

'Father Cassidy, I have made up my mind.'

'I tell you what. I have a lot of paper-work, now I'm on this committee of Sir Alfred's, as you can see.'

He threw a few magazines across the table.

'You can help me with that for a while. In fact, why not come along to the Gobi Club tonight, and see the committee in action? Sir Alfred's chauffeur is coming to pick me up at ten o'clock. Wear civvies, of course. It wouldn't do to be seen in a place like that in a clerical collar. Now run along, now, and get ready.'

Norman had no time to reply. Not even the chance to remind the Father Provincial of his suggestion that they say Vespers together. He was soon got rid of. When the door had closed, Father Cassidy reached for the telephone and dialled a number in Fleet Street.

Norman went back to his room with a couple of the porno-graphic journals under his arm. He put them on his desk, removed a pipe from the rack, took off his shoes, and lay on the bed.

The room was depressingly small, and painted cream. It had a bed, a desk, a small wash-basin, a prie-dieu and a chair. The only ornamental features were a crucifix from Oberammergau which he had rescued from the broom cupboard, and a photograph of his father, taken during the war, wearing a Colonel's uniform and a helmet, inspecting an anti-aircraft gun. When the pipe was lit, he lay back and gave himself over to melancholy.

There would have been a time when the notion of an evening at the Gobi Club would have provided him with some amusement. Now, it seemed as depressing as everything else: the retreat, Lubbock, the prospect of Christmas, or the intractable attitudes of Father Cassidy. It all felt so unreal, and it had been going on for so long. He had never really thought of himself as a priest. Now, apparently, he was doomed to remain one, growing aged and dull, like some of the insufferable old bores who pottered around the corridors of the house.

The difficulty partly sprang, he saw, from the nature of the Institute itself. Other religious orders in the church had a fairly clear view of what their function in life was. Presumably, if one joined one of these, it was plain sailing. Carthusians were hermits who spent all day gardening. Dominicans were left-wing academics. The Oratorians were retired Anglican clergymen. The Benedictines made wine or ran boarding schools for the sons of the middle classes. You knew where you were with them. The Catholic Institute of Alfonso had no such clearly defined position in the life of the church. It, too, ran schools and parishes. There was even a college at Cambridge, Martyr Hall. But, apart from the generalized aim of interfering in everyone else's affairs, there was nothing specific about the Alfonsine vocation. Every member of the Institute was meant to be a specialist of one sort or another. To hear Father Cassidy talk, one would have thought that every singular production of human genius, from the colonization of the New World to the splitting of the atom, had come about as the result of the efforts of one or another member of the order.

Norman wondered whether they would let him go back to Cambridge for a period of study. He had enjoyed reading history. He could not see what possible harm could come from spending a few years at Martyr Hall writing a thesis. But he knew, from the way Father Cassidy had said he would not be happy about such an arrangement, that it would never be allowed.

It would have been nice to become a student again. He would probably be able to pass himself off as a layman and spend most of his time in other colleges. By the time the thesis was finished, he could perhaps have drifted away from the Institute altogether; met a girl; got married . . .

28

He groaned. Father Cassidy doubtless anticipated all these things too. When Norman had joined the order, his emotional entanglements with the opposite sex were so intense and painful that he imagined he would never be happy until he rid himself of them irrevocably. The vow of chastity was, from his point of view the most attractive thing about the life of a Catholic priest. But, with the passage of time, he had found out that he was wrong. It was not feelings of lust which made this clear to him so much as the lassitude, irritation, boredom which were brought on by living in an all-male community. There were so many things he missed about regular female companionship, apart from sex. Nice cooking, humorous conversation devoid of banter, an enjoyment of the way things looked. The nuns in Father Sporran's *entourage* hardly seemed like women at all in those terms.

Going to the Gobi Club would, presumably, awaken a sexual appetite which he had fairly well under control. But it could hardly provide any of the delights of female companionship which he was actively missing.

He smoked pensively. A very odd thing was happening. He felt himself turning to gooseflesh. There was a shiver passing down his spine. That rarest of things, a brilliant idea, was forming itself in his brain. It was so brilliant that he wondered why he had never thought of it before. It had a Napoleonic simplicity. If Father Cassidy would not allow him to leave the Institute voluntarily, he must behave in a way calculated to make them give him the sack. What better place to start than a notorious night-club in Soho? A few carefully timed acts of indiscretion in full view of Sir Alfred Toogood and everyone else would surely lead to his instant suspension. If not, he could follow it up for the next few days with some more outrageous behaviour – shoplifting perhaps; a sermon at Sunday Mass attacking the Pope? an ill-judged letter to *The Times* about Ireland; he would be home and dry.

He stood up and stretched his arms. It would all be over in a matter of weeks. He could go and stay with his father. He was uncertain where the old man was at the moment, but it should be possible to find out. The end was in sight.

2

THE GARISH DAY

At five to ten, in a black clerical suit and a Roman collar, Norman waited in the hall for Father Cassidy to appear. His plans were complete. He had tanked up on a good deal of whisky, and was intending to start a lewd conversation with Sir Alfred Toogood in the car, before they even reached the Gobi Club. If that did not force the Father Provincial to reprimand him, he would try more extreme measures later in the evening.

The clock by the statue of the order's founder, Saint Alfonso of Barcelona, was striking ten when a lay brother came to tell him that Sir Alfred was at the door.

'I am still waiting for Father Cassidy,' said Norman.

'Father has asked me to tell you, Father, that he won't be coming with you this evening after all.'

'But I thought . . .'

'He has to be up early tomorrow to say mass for the Ursuline sisters.'

'I know. But he distinctly said . . .'

Hurried footsteps in the corridor interrupted this incoherent exchange, and Lubbock came round the corner, wearing a dirty mackintosh that looked as if it had been specially designed for frequenting nightspots of an unsavoury character.

'Come on, Shotty, we'll be late,' he said.

'We?'

'It's just struck ten.'

'I know. I've been here five minutes.'

Lubbock had him by the arm, and was escorting him to the front door.

'We're meant to be going incognito,' he added. 'Haven't you got an old coat or something you could put over that?'

'No,' said Norman.

It was intolerable that Lubbock should yet again be spoiling things. Still, it would not alter the poor impression which Norman intended to make on the rest of the party.

A chauffeur stood on the kerb outside and ushered them into the Daimler. Sir Alfred Toogood – his face familiar to Norman from his many television appearances – sat on the back seat, wearing an old trilby hat and an ulster which looked like a dressing-gown.

'Ah Fathers. How very good to see you.'

'Father Cassidy was unable to come,' said Norman, when he had introduced himself.

'He telephoned me earlier in the evening,' said the baronet. 'He is a busy man, and I quite understand. These disgusting places stay open so very late. And, believe me, the Gobi Club is *most* disgusting.'

'Good,' said Norman.

Sir Alfred blinked disconcertedly and the Daimler glided off through the frosty night. In the well-lit Mayfair streets, Norman was able to make out the innocent, donnish features of his companion; his slightly sensual mouth given a fanatical character by the way in which lower lip and jaw protruded.

'This is Father Lubbock,' said Norman.

'Father Lubbock and I are old friends,' said Sir Alfred.

Lubbock was burbling. Something about 'orphans'.

'And your name again, Father?'

'Shotover.'

'But everyone calls him Shotty,' said Lubbock, this time quite audibly.

'Then I shall do the same, if I may,' said the baronet.

Norman had half a mind to tell him that he mightn't; that no one but Lubbock used this ludicrous abbreviation; that if he heard it again, he would scream, be sick, commit murder. But he kept silence.

In the peculiar way which London has of setting totally different districts next to one another, Mayfair was scarcely quitted before the Daimler was squeezing its way into the brightly lit, noisy thoroughfares of Soho.

'We shall never be able to park here, sir,' said the chauffeur.

'Drop us on the corner of Berwick Street, Rowell. We can easily walk from there.'

The car pulled up by a shop called LOVEMAKING which appeared, from the wares advertised in the window, to sell moulds for making candles. Sir Alfred pointed it out to the two priests in passing with a despondent shrug, and led them off with the air of one who knew every inch of the streets they were traversing.

In spite of the frosty weather, there were lots of people about. Young men that Norman's father would have called dagoes lolled in every doorway, their street cries advertising a range of diversions, literary, cinematographic and sensual.

'Hey, sir, you like a very nice, young virgin?'

'Take no notice, Shotty,' said Sir Alfred.

'How much?' Norman asked.

'If you stop and talk to all of them we shall never get to the Gobi Club before the show starts.'

'Hey, sir, my friend. You leave your friend here with me. I fix him up with a very nice girl. Fifteen pounds. Ten pounds for her. Five pounds for me.'

'But I don't want you,' said Norman. 'I only want the girl. Ten pounds isn't very much for a virgin. What's the matter with her?'

Lubbock and Toogood bustled him away and, in spite of his efforts to linger in the 'bookshops', catch glimpses of blue movies, or dive into what purported to be sauna baths, the destined spot was eventually reached.

'Ah, Jonquil,' said Sir Alfred. 'I'm sorry if we have kept you.'

Two figures stood in the doorway of the Gobi Club. One, a plump but magnificent woman in late middle age, was Jonquil Yates, the famous mystic. The other turned out, surprisingly, to be a friend of Norman's from the old days, the Dundee of Caik.

32

'This is Father Lubbock and . . . er . . . Shotty,' said Sir Alfred, completing the introductions.

'How very extraordinary,' said the Dundee. He and Norman lingered in the doorway before following the others in. 'I thought you were an RC clergyman these days.'

'I am.'

'That's why you are dressed like that, I suppose?'

'Yes.'

'The RCs don't hold with sex shows, do they?'

'No. That's why Sir Alfred is coming here.'

'I can't tell whether I do or I don't. I'm not RC, of course. Do you think I should be?'

'No.'

'Toogood is. He's a sort of cousin of mine. Well, of my mother's. That's why he asked me along. He said he wanted the opinion of the younger generation.'

'But how nice to see you, Mungo. It's such ages.'

Meeting his old friend again brought feelings of warmth and joy that he had almost forgotten could be experienced.

'Since you became RC in fact. As I say, I used not to hold with RCs. Now I don't know. Another cousin of mine is an RC clergyman called Sporran. Have you heard of him?'

'He conducted our Christmas retreat this year.'

'His brother is very grand – the Sporran of Gorse. I haven't met the padre. He's a friend of that woman, apparently. She was talking about him rather a lot before you arrived. Who is she?'

'Mrs Jonquil Yates. She is a famous mystic.'

'She spoke to me without any introduction. Rather extraordinary, wasn't it? She just climbed out of a taxi and said I must be Mr Dundee, and that we were going to spend the evening together. In this part of London, one just doesn't know. Particularly when they wear all that make-up.'

There was a certain justice in Mungo's assessment of Mrs Yates's appearance. Although plainly a person who was going about doing good, she had something of the blowsy barmaid about her; almost, of the tart with the heart of gold. Perhaps it would be more accurate to say that she exuded the atmosphere of the fairground, a whiff of that quality which makes fortune-tellers seem like madams from a brothel. Giving off a great quantity of sweet scent, she strode ahead of them into the recesses of the club.

'Do you think we should have come?' asked the Dundee of Caik. 'I simply can't make up my mind.'

In so many ways, Norman felt it was nice to see his old friend again. Mungo was one of those people who always remain doggedly themselves, the reverse of chameleon in temperament; the incongruity or unlikelihood of his surroundings only increasing his self-parodying sameness. Nonetheless, his presence on this particular occasion made things awkward. Misbehaving in a night-club was going to be embarrassing enough, without having to do so in front of the man who had lived on the same staircase as himself for two of his three years at Cambridge. For all that, he was determined to do it.

Lubbock, re-emerging from the club, came up to them where they were dawdling in the entrance and said that Sir Alfred was already seated at his customary table.

'I thought we'd lost you, Shotty,' he said, in that excruciating imitation of good-humoured *badinage*.

'No such luck,' said Norman.

Sir Alfred Toogood sat at the table in the corner with a glass of lemonade and an open notebook in front of him. He looked as if he was about to judge a fancy dress competition at the village fête. Mrs Yates appeared less incongruous in that setting than he did. The pink lights catching her spectacles gave her something of the look of a sybil, pregnant with celestial fire. Her well-permed hair, blue in the daylight, took on a purplish tinge. She was wearing a black woollen shawl that had been crocheted for her by an admirer of one of her books — *The Inward Journey*. Her plain, rather massive face, with its very bright lips and rounded cheek-bones, seemed to be fixed on some infinitely sad, infinitely distant prospect which she alone possessed the spiritual maturity to look upon.

In fact, what was spread before them was a rather

34

crowded, smoky room which someone had taken the crudest and cheapest way of converting into an oriental lair. A plastic palm tree wilted in one corner. Beaded curtains hung in all the doorways, which had sellotaped on to them cardboard arches of vaguely mandarin proportions. A mural painting, just about recognizable as an allusion to the Willow Pattern, took up one wall, but most of the other walls were decorated with looking-glasses. A tiny stage, brightly spotlit, rose up at one end of the room.

As if to enliven these dispiritingly unsuccessful attempts to render the lure of the East, the management had hung up a few Christmas decorations, and the waitresses, mostly Chinese girls in bikinis, had pieces of tinsel in their hair.

Two or three of them had advanced on Sir Alfred's table. One sat on his knee, while the other made improper suggestions to Lubbock. A third came round to Norman and Mungo Dundee.

'You two boys feeling lonely, yes?'

'No,' said Mungo.

'Would you like me to get you a drink?'

She had managed to stand in a way which made it inevitable that the slightest movement on either Norman's part or Mungo's would involve stroking her thighs.

'Perhaps a glass of whisky,' said Norman. There was nothing objectionable in feeling this silky yellow flesh against the back of one's hand; but Mungo sat back in a frozen position which suggested immediate awareness that any physical contact with the waitress would be answered for on the bill at the end of the evening.

'How much is the whisky?' he asked cautiously.

'Five pounds,' she said coyly.

'Well, I'm certainly not playing at that game.'

'I could help you drink it,' she giggled. It felt to Norman as if she was trying to undo his fly-buttons, but he was too nervous to look.

Mungo's sudden appearance on the scene, quite apart from the absence of Father Cassidy, looked as if it was going to stymie any efforts Norman made to disgrace himself that

35

evening. But he was still sober enough to recognize that he must do something: in fact, that his future depended on it.

'Two whiskies,' he said, smacking the waitress's bottom.

'You naughty boy,' she smiled, adding, 'your buttons are very stiff. We must try to get them open later on.'

'That's pretty forward, wouldn't you say?' said Mungo, when she had gone. 'And I never heard of whisky costing so much.'

Mrs Yates's eyes had filled with tears, either through holding them open for so long and so wide in a smoky atmosphere, or on account of some profound emotional stirring within herself. She seemed to be murmuring some incantation, curse or blessing, to invoke the presence of the spirits.

Norman caught the words, 'too awful'.

Her presence, too, in addition to Mungo's, was going to make bad behaviour, of the outrageous kind he had planned, rather difficult to pull off. In a peculiar way, she exuded amiability.

'What an awful, awful mess we have made of sex,' she said – this time more audibly, with her eyes still fixed on the distant corner of the room.

Norman was tempted to reply that this was what sex was *for*. But the words failed him. He said, 'Yes. We have.'

'Do you suppose we shall be able to stay when the show actually starts?' she asked.

'Perhaps we should,' said Norman.

'What a beautiful soul you have,' she said.

Sir Alfred leant across to ask him for a verbatim account of his conversation with the waitress. He wrote the word FLY-BUTTONS in his notebook.

'I've never heard of anything so disgusting,' he said.

'The girls look so young,' said Mrs Yates.

Her words were drowned by the clanging of a gong which announced the beginning of the entertainments. A young man came on to the little stage dressed in a mandarin's costume and accompanied by two girls in thigh-length boots.

They, too, in a curious way, Norman found inhibiting.

36

When the music started, and their ludicrously obscene performance began, he hardly knew where to put his face. He was not morally shocked so much as embarrassed on their behalf, and doubly embarrassed to be watching them in the presence of Mrs Yates. Besides, the behaviour of the rest of the committee was so distracting that, even if he had wanted to concentrate on what was being enacted under the spotlights, it would have been difficult to give it his fullest attention.

'Where do you think she's gone with those drinks? Do you think she thought we wanted to buy a whole bottle? Five pounds seems an awful lot to me . . .'

The Dundee of Caik's hesitant commentary on the evening's happenings kept up a steady flow on Norman's left. Mrs Yates kept drawing her breath and covering her face with her hands, while Sir Alfred said, 'Do look, Jonquil: they're doing it again. Really, this must be the most repulsive show in London. Something ought to be done about it.'

During a pause in the performance, the waitresses came back with some very small glasses of whisky, and a bottle of iced water.

'You like me to sit on you knee?' one of them asked.

'I don't call this five pounds' worth of whisky,' the Dundee protested.

'Perhaps you like five pounds' worth of something else?'

'But I ordered whisky.'

Another, who had removed her bra, was running her fingers through Norman's hair.

'Please don't do that,' he said.

'You no like?'

There was no need to reply to this. Lubbock, who had been sitting so quietly by Sir Alfred's side that Norman had almost forgotten his presence, leant forward and said, 'Come over here.'

His own waitress had evidently been more generous with her allowance of alcohol than the young woman attendant on Mungo Dundee, and she had momentarily left him to fetch yet another drink. Perhaps, without Norman's noticing the fact, Lubbock had already been fairly tight before the evening began.

Norman and Mrs Yates exchanged glances. Evidently, a 'scene' was about to take place.

'Come here,' Lubbock repeated.

The girl looked coy, unwilling, perhaps, to trespass on another waitress's patch.

'I'm going to have those knickers off you,' said Lubbock. 'Then you are going to have a good spanking.'

The careful way in which he enunciated the words made it abundantly clear that he was barely in control of himself.

'Steady on, Lubbock,' said Norman.

Sir Alfred began to look desperate. Lubbock had stood up, and was stretching across the table, upsetting a chair, and almost knocking off Mrs Yates's spectacles. The waitress gave a little scream, and hid behind Norman for protection, putting her arms around his neck.

'Come here,' said Lubbock. His face had a look of peculiar fierceness. He picked up a fork from the table and began to brandish it. Attention from other members of the audience was being drawn to the violent little tableau at Sir Alfred's table. A chinaman in a dinner-jacket was hurriedly advancing upon them, accompanied by a pair of burly men, obviously 'bouncers'.

It was at this moment, as the girl still clung to Norman for protection, that the flash-bulbs began to pop.

Sir Alfred looked up beneficently at the row of cameras which surrounded them. The performers from the stage had come down to make sure that they too were in the picture, and the manager was waving his arms in the air and threatening to call for the police.

'We live in a sick society,' said Sir Alfred to the reporters. 'This club, these poor young people, are merely symptoms of the fact.'

'Did you enjoy the show, Sir Alfred?'

'I thought it was the filthiest thing I have ever seen in my life.'

The manager took notice of the phrase and had it written

38

up in neon lights over the door the week after Christmas.

Lubbock was by this stage under the table in a state of semi-consciousness. Everything had happened so fast that Norman could hardly take it in at all. On one level, it seemed too good to be true. Actually to be photographed in the garb of a Roman Catholic priest, clutching a naked girl in a night-club, in the midst of a drunken brawl, was better than he could have engineered for himself. But the presence of Mrs Yates and Sir Alfred made it less unambiguously disgraceful. Mrs Yates unpeeled the girl from his shoulders and spoke to the reporters, while Norman and Mungo tried to persuade Lubbock to stand up. It was just as well that Sir Alfred's chauffeur was on call to take them all home.

When Norman awoke the next morning, it was Lubbock's behaviour which came first to mind. It explained so much about the man – his vagueness, his inability to keep time, his egotistical and highly developed fantasy life – to learn that he had a weakness for the bottle. At the same time, Norman felt that it was typical of Lubbock that he could not go to a night-club without drawing attention to himself.

Still, in the general scheme of things which Norman had evolved, the evening could have done nothing but good. The camera, after all, could not lie. Surely the fact that he was wearing a clerical collar, his *risqué* behaviour with the waitress, would help to put the nail in the coffin of his priestly career. Lubbock, through either good luck or cunning, had been under the table when the pictures were taken.

Norman rose, shaved, dressed, dived down to the church to say mass at the altar of St Thérèse de Lisieux, and returned to the refectory for breakfast. It was a morning routine which he had got down to a fine art and which he regularly accomplished within the space of half an hour.

When he had poured out some coffee for himself and cut two slices of brown bread, he opened a couple of daily papers. Luckily, all the newspapers were delivered to the Institute's house in Mayfair. But it was to the more vulgar ones that he turned first.

There he was. The tableau was most extraordinary. The Dundee of Caik and Sir Alfred were both sitting upright and staring into the camera, as if they were part of a team photograph for a school second eleven. Behind them, naked figures took postures so brazen that the newspaper had been obliged to blot out various parts of the picture with rectangles. Mrs Jonquil Yates was holding Norman's hand and gazing adoringly at his face. He had quite forgotten that. And the Chinese girl, whose nakedness was concealed by his shoulder, looked abject, innocent and frightened. Still, it could have been worse.

The headline was a little baffling: STRIPPER TAKES THE VEIL.

Pixie Moon, a hostess at Soho's notorious Gobi Club, last night told reporters of her intention of becoming a nun. This shock announcement came after she had been rescued from the advances of a dangerous rapist by a Catholic priest. The priest, Father Norman Shotover, known to his friends as 'Shotty', had gone to the club as a member of Alfred Toogood's fact-finding mission into vice and corruption in London's West End. A spokesman said last night: 'Father Shotover's work is well known. He showed great physical courage and compassion.'

Throwing down the newspaper in amazement and despair, he tried another.

SHOTTY SAVES GIRL FROM VICE RING, read one headline. ' "He showed me that God loves me," said Soho stripper Pixie Moon . . . '

Even the more serious newspapers had got hold of this wildly distorted story.

The Founder of the Christian religion extended his message to outcasts, prostitutes and sinners. All too often the Christian Church has forgotten this vitally important

40

task. But in every generation, a few brave men and women show by their example the meaning of forgiveness. 'Shotty' Shotover, the young Alfonsine priest, is such a man . . .

Sipping his coffee in silence, Norman wondered how his plan could have so badly misfired.

'Well, it's good to see that you've found some work that suits you.'

Father Cassidy's hard tones, his pudgy blank expression, interrupted Norman's perusal of the newspaper.

'Good morning, Father.'

'I thought the leader in *The Times* was very sensible, very fair.'

He could hardly think otherwise, since he had dictated it himself.

'It's all a mistake,' said Norman. 'I don't believe that waitress wants to be a nun at all.'

'I wouldn't be so sure about that,' replied the Provincial. 'It's all very good publicity for the Institute anyway, thanks be to God.'

'But I can't have converted her. I merely asked her for two whiskies, and . . . '

'Ah! AND. Too modest, my boy, that's your trouble. It was probably that AND which did it.'

He moved off through the refectory at a brisk pace, whistling gently through his teeth and looking as pleased as Punch.

As Norman helped himself to toast and marmalade, it came to him that it was all Lubbock's fault. If Lubbock had not been there, it would have been he, Norman, whose drunken behaviour would have attracted notice. As it was, because he was not actually waving forks about and collapsing under tables, people had assumed that he was sober, and mistaken his flirtation with the waitress as missionary endeavour. It was all highly peculiar.

When he got back to his room, he realized that something had to be done. A new plan had to be devised which would get him thrown out of the Institute. He decided at once on

41

two courses of action. He would preach a very offensive Christmas sermon, and he would spend the remaining shopping days before that stealing things in Bond Street and Oxford Street.

He went upstairs and began his preparations. He had not written more than a few sentences of his homily on the Papacy, and was just changing 'bumbling' to 'prurient', 'obstinate' to 'pig-headed', when the telephone rang.

It was the first of many calls that day. One of the conversations was recorded and broadcast for the one o'clock news. Another was from the BBC religious affairs correspondent, asking him to make a special programme about night-clubs. The others were all editors, asking him to write articles, give interviews, or consent to be photographed.

He could not understand it. It exhausted but it also excited him. He had become mildly famous, and it was a very nice feeling indeed. It no longer seemed to matter that the things he was quoted as having said in the night-club were untrue. It gave him pleasure now to repeat them.

He even wondered whether he should continue with the anti-papal sermon. But while considering the question the telephone rang once more.

'Shotty, dear, it's Jonquil.'

'Jonquil?'

'Jonquil Yates.'

'Oh, yes.'

'I'm so pleased by all the coverage you've been having. Freddie is, too. He's going to have you on his programme, if you'll consent to be on it.'

'Freddie?'

'Freddie Toogood.'

'Oh, yes.'

Toogood's discussion programme, 'Who Cares?', was a regular feature of Sunday evening viewing. In the days when he watched a lot of television, Norman had always regarded it as a cue for having a bath. Nowadays he was usually in church at the hour when it went on the air, but he had rather assumed that it had been replaced by something else.

'We must meet for lunch one day. I can tell you all about it. And I want to have your opinions about astral bodies.'

Her cooing voice sounded sensual and remote through the receiver. It was not inconceivable that she was actually addressing Norman from 'the other side'.

'That would be very nice.'

'That and other things,' she said. 'I'm so glad that we have become friends.'

Christmas, in the event, passed without incident. Norman's room became cluttered with the things he had stolen from the shops, but, however hard he tried to draw attention to his shoplifting, nobody took any notice. He now found himself possessed of a cine-camera, two fur coats, a pair of skis, half a dozen memoirs of the Mitford family, three boxes of cigars, a child's tricycle and a golfing umbrella. He had felt sure, as he waved these conspicuous items under the noses of shop-assistants, and ostentatiously blundered his way through revolving doors with them, that he would be apprehended by a store detective, but he had no such luck. He decided not to repeat the experiment in the January sales. There was no more room to put the things; and besides, when he came to think of it, he might find himself being put in prison, which would probably be even less agreeable than life in the Institute's Mayfair house.

He wrote his anti-papal sermon and was ready to preach at the Midnight mass. At the last moment, however, he found that he was not 'down' for the Midnight after all. Lubbock preached a completely incoherent homily on the subject of shepherds seeing apparitions, which included a story of an ancestor of his who had once seen a ghost in Bamburgh.

Knowledge that Lubbock was alcoholic – in at least some senses of that term – did not make him any easier to live with, even if it vaguely helped to explain things.

Norman wondered if Father Cassidy knew about it and, if so, whether anything was to be done. The baffling thing about it was that, since the evening at the Gobi Club, Lubbock had not shown the faintest sense that he had behaved badly. Nor did he appear to have noticed that the incident had attracted a good deal of publicity. It was as if there was a conspiracy of silence over the issue. The only thing which appeared to interest anyone about the evening was that it had launched Norman's career. Pixie Moon, incredible as it seemed to Norman, really had enlisted with Father Sporran's dancing nuns. The requests for interviews, stories, and contributions to periodicals and broadcasts, looked like coming in a steady trickle for a few more weeks at least.

Norman could now see that Alfonsine priests, on the whole, fell into two categories, the public and the private. Those not favoured by the Provincial, thought of as dullards, who were pretty quickly found work in parishes, or forced to become dons; and the other category, the bright boys, who became journalists, poets, politicians, men of affairs.

Norman had never hoped, once these distinctions had begun to dawn on him, that he would be anything but one of the dullards. They, on the whole, were the men in the Institute that he actually *liked*. Their life-styles were less noisy and they were conspicuously more intelligent. Martyr Hall was full of them. And all the more agreeable masters of Rockthorpe, the famous Alfonsine school, came under this heading, too. It was when he became reconciled to the fact that he could not adapt himself to *their* way of life that Norman decided that he would have to leave the order. Now he found himself being unwillingly thrust into the other camp, with the trendies and the publicists, it was difficult to know what to do.

Difficult, too, was to know where Lubbock fitted into all this. Clearly he thought of himself as a sort of *éminence grise* analogous to Father Cassidy himself. But, as Norman was beginning to discover, how one thought of oneself in the Institute was not of the slightest consequence. The important thing was what Father Cassidy and the hierarchy thought. Norman had a very dim sense – no more than a hunch – that Lubbock, alcohol or no alcohol, played a part in their schemes. But it was quite impossible to know what, or how.

Fascination with Lubbock's character – the ultimate compliment one could pay to his egotism – was something which occupied most of Norman's waking thoughts when he was not consciously plotting to get himself the sack.

How could Lubbock be at once a bore and an object of fascination; a dyspeptic, and a man who could eat three helpings of cold Christmas pudding on Boxing Day; an introvert and a neurotic extrovert; a man Norman hated, and yet, in a totally inexplicable way, a man whom it was impossible to dislike?

So, Christmas passed. It was always faintly pathetic in institutional surroundings, like a fulfilment of the nightmare that one would have to spend Christmas at school. Norman could tolerate the institutional sides of it perfectly well. He had, after all, having been educated in a traditional middle-class way, spent most of his life in institutions, and away from whatever could be called 'home'. It was the intrusions of home into all this that he found intolerable. Father Cassidy in a paper hat. Pulling crackers with the Bursar. These things made one want to weep, almost more than the cards and presents from the outside world.

Since the abolition of the ten-shilling note, Colonel Shotover had been at a loss as to what to send Norman as a Christmas present. But one of his lovely hand-made cards had arrived on Christmas Eve. His new address, in flowing italic calligraphy, was inscribed on the back: *The Martello Tower, near Wimbridge on Sea, Dorset*. A note was enclosed. *I bought this place for an absolute snip. It has a big room which I am using as a studio, which looks out to the Channel. The oast house wasn't fit to live in. The man who built it wants shooting. All the best for next year . . .*

3

PRIDE RULED MY WILL

Jonquil Yates was formidable in appearance. But never having seen her outside the subdued artificial lights of the Gobi Club, Norman had not fully taken in the oddity of the full ensemble until they met, a week or two after Christmas, in an Italian restaurant on the edges of Bloomsbury.

She had telephoned several times to confirm this luncheon date, reiterating that she wished to discuss astral bodies, and 'other matters', and calling Norman 'Shotty, dear' every other sentence. Her resonant tones had somehow transcended the prosaic medium of the telephone receiver on each occasion that she rang; so that, even had Norman been engaged on the day she suggested, there would have been no question of refusal.

Norman did not know much about astral bodies; nor even, to borrow the Dundee of Caik's way of thinking, whether he ought to hold with them. But they made a pleasant change from the pornographic magazines. Father Cassidy had put him in charge of bestialism and bottoms, and he was becoming weary of the endless pictures of people and their animals.

A very strong, icy wind blew up Charlotte Street and there was sleet in the air before he reached Giuseppe's. Mrs Yates sat at a table near the window. If it had not been such a bleak day, Norman would have assumed that she was sitting in pools of sunshine. The fact that the harsh rays were electric did not diminish the impression that, in a magical way, she attracted light, possibly even exuded it. Nor were her clothes – an orange wig, swathed in chiffon, falling on to sleeveless shoulders – suggestive of the English winter which surrounded her.

He did not recognize her at first. It was not merely that the wig had changed colour. There was something elusive about her features, at once soft and firm; sensual and vaguely mannish. It was a handsome face; a good bone structure of forehead, cheeks and jaw well swathed in flesh. Her cheeks were covered in the very faintest down, heavily powdered, which stood out in the clear artificial light. When Norman approached her table, her features creased into a smile.

'Mrs Yates.'

'Jonquil,' she corrected him firmly. Rather to his surprise, she stood up and kissed him. It was a delightful, lingering kiss, full of scent and softness.

'I feel I am here under false pretences,' he said. 'I really know very little about . . . '

She touched her lips with a forefinger to bring his sentence to an end.

'They are very close to us,' she cooed. 'We must be careful what we say.'

'They?'

'I hope that you like Italian food,' she continued in a brisk, matter-of-fact tone of voice. 'There is a fairly wide range of dishes.'

'I love it.'

'I knew you did.' Her tone suggested either the possession of second sight in relation to Norman's eating habits or, more likely, control of an intelligence service which could put her in touch with such information. Then she added, 'I have been coming here since 1934.'

How old was she? It was impossible to say. That she was under forty was unthinkable, but Norman was surprised that she was old enough, assuming that she began to frequent Giuseppe's in adult life, to have been doing so for forty years.

They ordered salami and olives, followed by Vitello Verbena with Tagliatelle. A bottle of Frascati, not particularly good, brought pleasant memories of a holiday in Perugia with Mungo.

'Tell me about yourself, Shotty,' she said, when talk about the food had fizzled out.

'I hardly know what to say.'

'Then let *me* tell you about yourself.'

She made sweeping gestures with a noodle.

'You are a soul in prison.' The hint of a Welsh accent added to the musical quality of her voice when in incantatory tone. 'Like all followers of the way, you feel shut in, trapped, a wild thing locked in a cage, a stranger marooned on foreign shores . . .'

'Does it show?'

'Of course it does.'

She sipped her Frascati and fixed him with her large watery eyes.

'It is a wonderful thing to be a priest,' she said.

'It's a job, like everything else.'

'So wrong! You deny your virtues! Of course, for most men who are priests, the true nature of their calling remains for ever hidden, veiled, obscured. Then, for one man in a thousand, the veil is lifted. He sees behind the form to the reality of things.'

'He does?'

She took his hand, and leant forward so that their noses were nearly touching.

'I think that what you did that evening in that night-club was one of the most beautiful acts I have ever seen a man perform. It was like something in Spenser.'

'What was?'

'Shielding that poor mistaken girl from the eyes of the camera. Seeing so clearly her limpid qualities of soul. Father Sporran says that she will make a very good nun.'

Norman felt that things were falling into place. It must have been Mrs Yates who had given his 'story' to the news-papers.

'It is very kind of you to say so.'

'It is not kind. It is *true*.'

'Did Pixie Moon want to become a nun?'

Mrs Yates smiled. Though she was so different in character, temperament, demeanour, bearing, from Father Cassidy, Norman could see analagous symptoms of

48

dominance in her facial expression. It was the self-confident smile of one who was in love with power and knew how to exercise it. Father Cassidy exercised his will over his victims by an apparent detachment from the emotions. Mrs Yates did so by inebriating them with sentiment and flattery.

'She will make an excellent nun,' she repeated. 'And Father Lubbock agrees with me.'

'Lubbock?'

This was very puzzling. Norman could just see how his own demeanour in the Gobi Club could be distorted into a picture of gallant behaviour. Lubbock's grovelling under the table in a drunken stupor was less easy to view in such heroic lights. Why then, was he consulted about the advisability of Pixie Moon's taking the veil – or, rather, the gym-slip?

'Father Lubbock is a sick man,' she said, as if he had been thinking aloud, and she had prepared the reply.

This had been one of Father Cassidy's lines. Now that Norman knew the nature of the 'illness', he found the topic distasteful.

'He bears his illness well, bravely. But he is also an acutely sensitive person. Whether he is a good priest or not, I cannot tell.'

'No.'

He had come to the restaurant steeled to the idea of discussing astral bodies and spiritual life. But he had not reckoned on these tedious and infinitely extensible investigations into Lubbock's psyche.

'So you think so, too? You have noticed his struggles?'

'Since you mention it, I don't think he is a very good priest, no.'

'Would you say that he and I are kindred spirits?'

'I haven't really thought about it. I don't know either of you very well.'

She leant back and sighed.

They had reached the coffee stage. She produced some cheroots from a handbag, offered one to Norman, which he refused and lit up herself.

'Father Lubbock has told me so much about you,' she

said. 'He says that you are the only priest in the community that he can really relate to, that he would really call a *friend*. I expect that you feel the same about him.'

There was no answer to this. Norman felt that the conversation had left him miles behind as soon as the name of Pixie Moon had been mentioned. Mrs Yates's view of things differed so violently from his own that it was difficult to know where to start. He decided to sit quiet and let her talk wash over him in syrupy waves. An alliance between herself and Lubbock was the last thing that he would have expected.

'Have you known Lubbock long?' he asked at length.

She was silent momentarily. She smiled once more, letting out clouds of smoke through her mouth and nostrils so that for a while she was lost in a blue haze, like some half-embodied spirit. Perhaps it was this which led Norman's thoughts back to the astral plane.

'As I said before,' she said, 'it does not do to speak too freely on the subject. There are many spirits abroad, and not all of them benign. You have perhaps heard that I am on the Archbishop of Canterbury's committee to investigate the subject. They needed someone who knew about it from the *inside*.'

At the mention of the word *committee*, she adopted a new voice. It seemed to come from deep down in her chest as if a genie, rather a self-important one, was being released from the depth of her lungs.

Clearly, once one became accustomed to sitting on committees, there were an endless number to claim one's attentions. Norman had heard of this one. It was extraordinary that she found the time to produce her steady torrent of books, she sat on so many of them. They were mostly organized by one ecclesiastical authority or another. Norman did not know to what church, if any, she herself belonged. Sir Alfred Toogood's anti-pornographic activities and Father Sporran's dancing nuns represented her Catholic interests. He had seen her picture in the newspaper the previous week, standing with an archimandrite of the Russian Orthodox Church outside the Brighton Pavilion.

Now there was this sinister-sounding Anglican committee.

'They know so little of these things. Exorcism, spirits, voices from the other side . . .'

'Black magic?'

'What they call black magic.' She smiled cryptically. 'I wonder if you would like to be on the committee.'

'I hardly think I would have the time. Besides, if it is organized by the Archbishop of Canterbury, he might not take kindly to a Catholic priest . . .'

'That's just where you are wrong. The terrible old barriers between man and man, church and church, are being broken down. Not by the machinations of the bureaucrats, but by the free working of the Spirit. That is what Father Sporran has taught us all. That, in a different way, you too can teach us.'

She was sailing off into fantasy again. He did not know what she was talking about.

'Freddie is frightfully keen on you, by the way,' she resumed.

'Sir Alfred?'

'Yes. He is longing to have you on "Who Cares?" There is going to be a programme in a fortnight's time about authority in the church. I told him that it was just your cup of tea. So he will probably be getting hold of you in the next few days.'

'But I don't know anything about authority in the church.'

She squeezed his hand, and her eyes filled with tears.

'So modest,' she murmured. 'Such a dear, pure, self-effacing soul . . .'

Peeling off the false nose and moustaches, Father Cassidy flinched with momentary pain. He had eaten too much spaghetti and was feeling irritable. Why did the confounded woman always have to eat in that Italian restaurant?

He had disliked most things that he had heard, particularly the rubbish about breaking down the barriers between man and man. He was in business to keep them up; if possible, to erect a few more. Well-meaning fanatics like Sporran needed watching. He made a note of the fact in his diary. *The pyjamas*

51

need to go to the laundry he wrote, erasing it and translating it into Polish to be on the safe side.

Nor did he like the talk of his priests being souls in prison wanting to escape. As he made clear, to anyone who asked, no member of the Institute was obliged to stay any longer than he wanted. Plenty were leaving, vulgar publicists who could do no harm, most of them. The ones with something up their sleeves, he made sure, were not allowed to escape.

He could not work Mrs Yates out. In his view of the world, there were only two sides, his own and the other. In many ways, he would have thought that she was on his own. But her assignation with young Shotover made him less certain. He wondered what they were really talking about when they referred to subjects with such obvious code-names as 'Astral bodies' or 'the Archbishop of Canterbury'.

Then there was the question of Shotover's television appearance. Toogood could be relied on, he had no doubt, but what would the young man do? It was a risk, until he could be absolutely certain of his ground. Sooner or later, the boy would slip up, show his hand. Then the Institute could pounce. Until then, it was as well to give him plenty of rope and let him hang himself.

He put some Sweetex in his coffee and turned his thoughts to the President of the Board of Trade.

Norman was now determined that nothing should go wrong, as on all the previous occasions. It was absolutely essential that he should bring unambiguous disgrace on himself and on the Catholic Institute of Alfonso.

He saw now that, even if Jonquil Yates had not spoken to the newspapers; even if he had not had the appalling bad luck to have happened on Pixie Moon, the notion of misbehaving in a night-club had been naïve. It could too easily look like a temporary aberration. And fornication was hardly the sort of thing that Father Cassidy would think of giving a man the sack for.

The obvious time and place for his next attempt was a television studio. Instead of a handful of inebriated witnesses in a darkened Soho bar, he would have the entire viewing public. No one would be able to mistake his words or deeds. But what should he do?

Once again, although he flinched at the prospect, he had considered some obscenity of behaviour or language. Taking down his trousers in the middle of *Songs of Praise*, perhaps. Then he thought again. Only a lunatic would behave like that. His object was release, not further confinement. To give the impression that he was bananas, cuckoo, off his chump, might lead to a change in his way of life, but it scarcely would lead to a change for the better. Besides, nowadays, anything could happen. There would bound to be some clergyman, perhaps even a member of his own order, inane enough to interpret even indecent exposure as a meaningful theological gesture. He needed, with such people about, to devise a plan which was foolproof.

By the time he reached the studio that Sunday evening, he had worked everything out to the last letter. There were to be three participants in the programme apart from Toogood himself: Norman, an Anglican clergyman of advanced modernist opinions, and some philosophy don, periodically dredged up by the BBC to express agnostic or atheist sympathies. Norman was meant to be defending the Roman Catholic position. In order to do so, he had been rehearsing the Christmas sermon he had never got round to preaching about the wickedness and absurdity of the Papacy. It was calculated to give offence to almost everyone, Catholic or non-Catholic. He could not see how it could fail. Within a matter of weeks, he thought with satisfaction, he would be back in civvies.

Freddie Toogood developed his brief in the bar before the rehearsal for the programme began. The baronet drank lemon squash and Norman had a gin and french.

'I can't very well show my hand, you see, Shotty, dear boy, because I'm supposed to be the chariman. But this Dean is a perfectly dreadful man. As far as I can see, he doesn't see the need for any authority in the church at all.'

'What do you think I should do?'

'Explain to him where we Catholics stand in relation to the Papacy, and why we believe it to be so essential. I know you have a thorough knowledge of theology since the Second Vatican Council. Father Cassidy told me so himself. You'll do it splendidly.'

Norman smiled and said that he would do his best. This was playing into his hands. When the Dean arrived, accompanied by the philosophy don, Norman realized that it was all going to be plain sailing.

The Dean of Selchester, a remote cousin of the Dundee of Caik's, was an acquaintance of Norman's from the old days, and they greeted each other warmly. Indeed, while Norman belonged to the Church of England, he had rather got into the habit of falling in love with the Dean's daughters.

The Dean himself was a mild-looking man who had made a career for himself by publishing heretical theology. His latest claim to fame had been to contribute to a volume of essays called *The Man Who Was Not God*, which attempted to demolish the idea of the Divinity of Christ and investigate such questions as the politics and sexual predilections of the Founder of the Christian religion.

'How are the family?' Norman asked.

'Well, thanks. I expect we shall have some hard talking,' said the Dean, rubbing his hands smugly. 'But I always maintain that real, honest, two-way dialogue is what true ecumenism is all about.'

'Quite so,' said Norman.

Sir Alfred cast his eyes up to heaven, and the philosopher smirked. He looked a stupid man, but even his circumscribed view of the world found it hard to stomach the Dean's zest for meaningless cliché. It was at Norman that his mean little eyes stared most maliciously. He knew how to demolish the papal claims without thinking. It was going to be a very enjoyable way of earning fifty guineas.

The programme started much more quickly than Norman had reckoned on. The rehearsal was very short, and he was careful not to give the game away during that. He spoke about the infallibility of the Pope and the miraculous

54

appearance of Our Lady at Fatima. But the make-up girl had no sooner powdered his brow than the theme-tune had started and Sir Alfred was leaning forward in his ugly Scandinavian chair and peering at the cameras.

It was hard to imagine, in the rather confined atmosphere of the studio, that millions of people, their TV suppers on their knees, were staring at him and listening to what they were saying. He did not feel in the least nervous.

'Good evening,' said the baronet. 'How often have we used phrases like *You shouldn't do that* or *You must do this; I ought to say that; I don't see why I shouldn't think that*. What is the basis for the moral statements that we make? What authority do we have for saying them? It is about authority that we are going to talk tonight. With me in the studio are Professor Gordon Hairbrush, Duns Scotus Professor of Moral Sciences in the University of Oxford; the Very Reverend Ron Hope, Dean of Selchester; and Father Norman Shotover, of the Catholic Institute of Alfonso. Professor, may I ask you first what you, as a philosopher, think is the place of authority in the moral life?'

Their voices droned on. Norman knew exactly what they were both going to say. They had already said it at the rehearsal. Hairbrush could not see any metaphysical authority for the moral statements that we make. The Dean could not either, but seemed to think this was a good moment for talking about a denomination know as the Caring Church. Toogood was a hopeless chairman. He let them talk far too much. Norman began to think that he would never get his word in.

'Your raising the subject of the church is very interesting,' he managed to say.

'The Caring Church,' the Dean corrected him. 'Basically, in order to be viable, the church has got to be, as I see it, an economically mature, politically active, caring community.'

'Father Shotover,' said Toogood. 'You are a Catholic priest.'

How awful the words sounded! How he longed for them not to be true!

'Yes,' he said carefully.

'Can I ask you what attitude you take to the question of authority in the church?'

The moment had come.

'Yes,' said Norman. 'You certainly can. In the Roman Catholic Church, you are supposed to believe in the authority of the Pope.'

Toogood nodded benignly. At last, in his view, someone was talking some sense.

'The Pope,' Norman repeated. 'Remember the bloke? Interfering old nitwit in a white dressing-gown; appears on a balcony from time to time and makes pronouncements about things he knows nothing about. In the old days, they used to burn effigies of the Pope in every English village on bonfire night. No bad idea. The sooner that fine old custom is revived the better, in my view.'

Toogood blinked. This was not what Norman had said at the rehearsals. It was all very perplexing. Professor Hairbrush looked even more crestfallen. He had been preparing a much milder version of the same speech himself in reply to what he had expected Norman to say. The Dean, however, never at a loss for words, burst in.

'What Norman is saying, of course, is very much in line with the new theology of authority which is being evolved in the Roman Church at the moment in places like Germany and Holland. As far as I can see, it is an entirely healthy development.'

'Is it?' asked Norman despairingly. 'Nitwit. I said the old fruitcake was a nitwit. Ga-ga. Past it. No good. No one listens to what he says, and when they do it is a disaster. Look at his teachings on birth control. What is he supposed to know about it?'

'Quite,' said the Dean. 'This is very much it. What you are saying is in line with some of the theology that has arisen in recent years out of the Dutch Catechism. Of course, you are still saddled with the outmoded concept of infallibility.'

'Yes,' said the philosopher, with the eager air of a drowning man clutching at a straw, 'what about infallibility? You are supposed to believe that the Pope is infallible, aren't you?'

Norman laughed contemptuously. He did not know how to pronounce the word PAH!, often read in books; nor did he know how to toss his head; but he made an attempt at doing both.

'If you believe that, you'll believe anything,' he said. 'The Pope is no more infallible than I am. Mind you, he has only made three infallible pronouncements, so-called, in the history of the papacy, you know. One to say that the Pope was infallible. The other two were rather obscure doctrines about the state and whereabouts of the Virgin Mary before and after her earthly life.'

'Perhaps,' said Freddie Toogood hurriedly, 'we can turn back to the Dean again for a moment . . . '

There was no more opportunity for Norman to talk during the programme. The Dean was discussing an area which he called the Third World, where viable and meaningful situations seemed to be cropping up all the time.

After the programme, Toogood looked tired and unhappy.

'Why did you do it, Shotty?' he asked.

'What?'

'Say all those things about the Pope.'

But Professor Hairbrush looked even more downcast. He offered Norman a cigarette.

'No thanks.'

Father Cassidy had warned him that even the most ordinary brands could be used to conceal hallucinatory drugs.

'You Alfonsines are as clever as a cartload of monkeys,' said the Professor.

Norman did not appreciate the implications of this remark until he triumphantly returned to Mayfair for what he took to be the last evening meal there. He assumed, rightly, that the Provincial would have seen the programme and would want an interview with him afterwards in his study.

'Very good, Norman, very good,' said Father Cassidy, when they were closeted together.

'What on earth do you mean?'

'Crudely done, perhaps, but shrewdly executed.'

The priest's spectacles glinted in the lamplight. Norman tried to discern from his expressionless features traces of anger, sarcasm or rebuke.

'I thought I could rely on you.'

'But . . .'

'No buts.'

'But not to attack the infallibility of the Pope,' said Norman hopefully.

'You didn't attack it. I already have a transcript of what you said. You explained what the doctrine was. You said that you were just as infallible as the Pope, which is true, unless he is making pronouncements *ex cathedra*. You made that perfectly clear. But you also made the point lightly and humorously. I liked the joke about the dressing-gown.'

'Surely not.'

'Oh, but I did. That's the sort of thing which will have won viewers round. Then, before they know where they are, they will find themselves becoming Catholics. That philosopher thought he was going to tie you up in knots. And, of course, he would have done, if you had stuck to some of the old-fashioned defences of the doctrine of infallibility. Instead, you anticipated all his arguments and took the wind out of his sails. And I like the way you emphasized that the English Province of the Institute is in the vanguard of modern theological thought.'

Norman still clung fretfully to the hope that this might be some cruel piece of sarcasm, some joke at his expense, before the Provincial suddenly pounced and told him that he was fired. But he enjoyed no such luck. Cassidy merely repeated his admiration for Norman's low cunning before dismissing the young man and turning back to a perusal of his sado-masochistic magazines.

Before going to bed, the Provincial added another entry to his notebook, this time in Sanskrit characters. *The rabbit still pretends that he likes radishes; but he is a sly little rabbit, and it will be difficult to get him in a trap.*

4

FAR FROM HOME

With the approach of Lent, Lubbock sank into a drinking bout of a scale too excessive to ignore. After one of his rare stints in the confessional, one of his penitents came to complain to the Provincial that she had been almost knocked back by the smell of whisky through the grille; and that, for her penance, Father Lubbock had told her to go and feed the ducks in St James's Park. He collapsed during Benediction on the following Sunday.

With his busy public life, Norman had seen much less of Lubbock in recent weeks, and, in consequence, was developing a sneaking affection for the man. He could not tell how this could be, since, when he came to analyse Lubbock's character, he still found every element of it quite as irritating as he had done before. Somehow, in a way which it was hard to explain, there was a sort of dignity about him when totally sloshed which was absent in his sober, cocky self. But, unquestionably, the strongest incentive to like Lubbock was that he now saw so little of him. He never came in to meals any more. Little trays containing milk puddings and boiled fish were taken up to his room by a kindly lay-brother, but they were usually returned uneaten. In spite of the Bursar's efforts to restrain any money supply in Lubbock's direction, he still managed – showing that his guile had not left him, even if all other rational faculties were gone – to get hold of drink by fair means or foul. When the simplest of the foul means was discovered – Lubbock's raid on the charity box for the Holy Souls at the back of the church – the Provincial was obliged to send him away from London.

Norman met him in the corridor on the morning of his

departure. He had lost a lot of weight and his face had become very blotchy. He must have been drinking heavily for several days on end.

'Hallo, Lubbock.'

'Eh?'

Lubbock stared up at him with frightened, bloodshot eyes.

'How are you?'

It would have been proper for Lubbock, on this occasion, to claim any degree of illness. He looked terrible. However, he simply stared about him wildly and burbled.

'What's that?'

'You've always been an old pal to me, Shotty.'

'Of course I have.'

'One of the best.'

'I hope so.'

'They're sending me away.'

'So I heard.'

'To that bloody little retreat house in Sussex.'

'I know. Well, you'll enjoy the rest.'

'God knows, I need it.'

He was crestfallen, crushed, and defeated. Norman felt a sinking feeling of awful waste as he looked into Lubbock's eyes. No one knew better than he how tiresome Lubbock could be. That hardly diminished the way in which his good qualities seemed to glow out of the wreckage which the drink had made of him. He *could* be companionable; he was, after a fashion, intelligent; witty . . . And thank God that he was going away.

Norman turned away and left Lubbock to shuffle off down the corridor. Presumably, if a few weeks at the retreat house were not enough to dry him out, more extreme measures would have to be resorted to; a psychiatrist, a clinic.

A few weeks before, all this would have given Norman food for thought; he too, could have feigned persistent drunkenness, and, sooner or later, he would have been sent away, suspended, put on the shelf or given the sack. But now, the thought did not even cross his mind. He had stopped thinking of ways in which to leave the Institute. With a bouncing, self-important step, he returned to his room and started to type an article for the *Tablet*.

Being photographed in a night-club with a naked waitress had done wonders for his career as a catholic priest; but that was as nothing to the effect of his comments on 'Who Cares?' about the infallibility of the Pope. He had become famous and popular almost overnight. The *Tablet* had taken it up at once, and its cautious tones had been enough to convey to him how important his utterance had been. It had a lot of sentences beginning with phrases like, 'even if we find ourselves unable to agree with all that Father Shotover says, it has to be admitted that . . . '

Of course, he did not notice how it had corrupted him; nor how his astonishing success had gone to his head. Nor did his original sense that it was all a put-up job, either by Father Cassidy or Mrs Yates, take long to wear off. He soon began to think that success meant talent, and that he must be a very clever young man indeed. He could hardly put a foot wrong. Everyone was clamouring to hear his views on everything, and he started to take on much more work than he could really do. In addition to his work on pornography, he found himself sitting on committees to discuss Birth Control, Liturgical Language, Torture, Homosexuality and the plight of Jews in the Soviet Union. And he was asked to preach in all the fashionable pulpits in London.

It meant repeating himself a good deal, but he fell more and more in love with the sound of his own voice. He found himself preaching his sermon attacking 'triumphalism' about six times a month and whenever he appeared on the television, he found himself saying the same things.

People seemed to have an endless appetite for it. The more pious the congregation, the more they seemed to like being told that old Catholic devotional habits were a waste of time; the more they relished being asked rhetorical questions such as 'What is the relevance, today, of the doctrine of the Assumption?' They lapped it up.

Trouble came on the first Sunday after Ash Wednesday.

Looking at his diary at about five o'clock in the afternoon, he suddenly noticed that he was meant to be preaching in the Cathedral at the evening Mass. It was an awkward moment. He could not very well ask about the relevance of the Assumption again. He had already asked it twice that day. And he did not want to spill any beans about what he had to say on the subject of contraceptive sprays, since he was appearing on a late-night discussion programme that very evening to examine the subject with a well-known inter-viewer.

There was only one thing to do, and that was to get a sermon out of a book. Plenty of people did it. Probably most priests did it all the time. He glanced hastily along the shelf. *The Pickwick Papers, Scouting for Boys* and *The Works of Shakespeare* would hardly provide anything very useful. He cursed himself for not building up more of a theological library. Then he recognized the name of Father Faber on the spine of an aged volume given him by the Dundee of Caik some weeks before. He flicked through its pages hastily. He could not remember who Father Faber was, but the book appeared to contain sermons, and one of them would have to do. Stuffing the book into a mackintosh pocket, he hurried out and caught a taxi.

Norman did not actually open the book until he was in the pulpit. There had simply not been time. The sea of faces beneath him induced the feeling, by now familiar, of dizzy self-congratulation. He wished that he had had the time to write something himself, but it could not be helped.

As he stood in the great marble pulpit, the splendid and mysterious Italianate architecture of Westminster Cathedral, its glimmering mosaics, its sturdy arches, its shadowy recesses and side-chapels, its glorious altar of the Blessed Sacrament ablaze with lights, meant nothing to him; but his words seemed to fit the scene well enough. Making the sign of the cross and opening the book at random, he began to speak. It was all a bit different from his own style, but it was in its own way elegant, and he was soon in his swing.

' . . . Day by day, hour by hour, all over the world, dear

brethren, the Precious Blood rains down upon the altars of Holy Church in one eternal and Catholic Oblation. Day by day, hour by hour, the prayers of the Coredemptrix, Our Most Blessed and Immaculate Mother Mary, are offered up for the sins of the whole world. These things are eternal, and will never change, just as the Holy Mass is eternal, and will never change. That is why, in his infinite Providence, the Holy Spirit of God has written indelibly the Holy Mass in the Latin tongue, so that all peoples and all nations may hear and offer the Holy Sacrifice in one language; just as they pray with one heart to one true and only God and Mary his mother . . .'

The words did not quite fit, as he realized while speaking them, since the Mass was not in Latin any more. But he did not suppose many people would notice. They came to hear *him*, and it did not much matter what he said. The whole thing had a rather rousing peroration about the Sacred Heart of Mary and the wickedness of the Jews.

Afterwards, in the sacristy, the other priests were distinctly stony. Norman was aware that they were muttering to themselves. No one had congratulated him on his sermon, as they usually did on these occasions. It was all decidedly peculiar.

He had time to return to Mayfair before going out again to Langham Place for his evening broadcast. As he bounced through the hall, a lay-brother stopped him and said that the Provincial wished to speak to him at once.

'Father Cassidy?'

'Yes Father.'

'But how tiresome. I've got to have a very hurried supper and then I'm dashing out to the BBC.'

'He said it was very important, Father.'

Norman swore, and knocked on Cassidy's door with some vigour. He felt that it was a complete cheek, the way the man asked to see him at such short notice and at such frequent intervals. He decided to give him a piece of his mind.

'Come in,' said Cassidy.'

The Provincial was sitting by the fireplace smoking a pipe

and perusing the *Financial Times* Share Index.

'Is this really necessary?' Norman asked. 'I've got to go out again in about half an hour.'

'Oh, yes?' Where is that?'

'To the BBC. I'm on the Late Show.'

'You won't be broadcasting tonight.'

'But I will. I'm going to be talking about contraceptive spray.'

'Are you deaf?' There was something almost offensive in the Provincial's tone. 'You won't be broadcasting tonight.'

'Why ever not?'

'I have rung up the BBC to tell them that you are ill. You can consider that you are suspended from your priestly duties until further notice. I shall have to be consulting a number of people first before we finally decide what to do with you.'

'But I don't understand.'

Almost instantaneously, the bumptious, cocksure patronizing demon who had come to possess Norman in recent weeks slipped away from him and was gone. It was like waking up after sleep. An incoherent, stammering young man stood before the Provincial.

'It was a clever move, Norman, but not quite clever enough.'

'I'm afraid I don't know what you mean.'

'You got yourself made a centre of public attention and approval. At first, I couldn't see what your motives were. It looked like simple conceit, so I did not interfere. But I still had my suspicions. I can now see that every move was very carefully planned.'

'What moves?'

'Your interest in pornography, the involvement in the charismatic movement, your seemingly radical views on the papacy. Now we see why you think so little of the present Pope. You whipped up public support for yourself, and then you pounced.'

All this was double-Dutch to Norman. He looked round the room to see if there was any evidence that Father Cassidy had been drinking.

'If I have upset you in any way, I apologize,' he said.

'All you were trying to do was get a platform for your divisive views.'

'Divisive?'

'There's no point in coming the innocent with me, Norman Shotover, or whatever you are really called. Ever since you arrived on the scene, I have known that you were up to no good. You have been plotting against the good interests of the Institute, and I won't have it.'

'You must have made some mistake . . . '

'Do I have to spell it out for you?'

'Yes.'

'You are one of the Tridentine Mass brigade, so called. I should have suspected it with all your early rising and your Trinity accent.'

'Tridentine Mass?'

'I should be interested to know how much they are paying you.'

'They?'

'There's no need to repeat everything I say in that innocent tone of voice, my lad. You know perfectly well what I mean.'

There was no point in continuing the conversation. Father Cassidy's paranoia could not be argued with.

Norman was packed off next morning to stay at the Institute's retreat house until further notice.

It did not take long, once he had subsided into his old self, and when he realized that a spell at the retreat house meant almost hourly contact with Lubbock, for the waves of irritation and depression to come sweeping back over Norman. Indeed, Lubbock was the first person he saw when he arrived in Sussex. He was slumped in a chair in the parlour, smoking a cigarette, and reading a newspaper. He greeted Norman enthusiastically.

'Shotty! How nice to see you. Come down for a bit of a rest?'

'You could say so.'

'Nothing wrong, is there?'

'I don't know.'

'They sent me here to dry out.'

'So I heard. How are you getting along?'

'I feel awful. Worse than ever. I think something has gone wrong with my intestines.'

'What does the doctor think?'

'He says that I'm getting better. None of them understand what I suffer.'

'I don't suppose that they do.'

Norman picked up the *Tablet* and sat down in the opposite corner of the room. He did not much want to discuss his own troubles, and he was in no mood to hear about the workings of Lubbock's internal organs.

'You know what they want to do with me, I suppose?' Lubbock continued.

'Who?'

'Cassidy. The big bosses.'

'No.'

'Send me off to South America.'

'I say!'

Norman checked himself. He hoped that the pleasure which this news gave him did not show. It was hard to suppress a faint note of glee. His brief spell of publicity had released him only momentarily from Lubbock and he had begun to think in a gloomy way that their destinies were everlastingly linked; that he was under a curse which he would carry about with him until he died. Now, there was hope that he was wrong.

'It would kill me, of course,' Lubbock added melo-dramatically.

'Do you really think so?'

Again, Norman hoped that no note of undue delight crept into his tone of voice.

'I've been all over South America, of course.'

Lubbock had assumed his bumptious, know-all voice.

'Oh, yes?'

'Me? Born in Rio. I must have told you.'

By now, Lubbock had been born in so many different

66

corners of the earth that Norman could not be bothered to keep track of them all.

'If I was going back for a rest cure, it wouldn't be so bad. Some of those luxury hotels in Rio are really something, I can tell you. But the shanty-towns will kill me.'

'So you said.'

'Mind you, I expect they thought that someone of my experience would be useful out there. In spite of all the rude things Cassidy said about me, he knows that I am a very good priest. You know that, too, don't you Shotty?'

'Of course.'

'I just don't understand why that woman complained about the way I heard her confession. I've never heard of anyone complaining before. As a matter of fact, I am a rather popular confessor. They used to wear me out, coming to ask my advice all the time . . .'

'I know.'

'Of course, not everyone can be famous, like some members of the Institute. Goodness knows, I'm not famous. I came up the hard way. I should never expect to be. But I do know my job.'

'Unquestionably. You will be marvellous in the shanty-towns.'

Norman did not see why he should not flatter Lubbock a little, if the end was really in sight.

'When are you going?' he asked.

'As soon as I've had all my injections. God knows if I am going to survive those. I'm allergic to practically everything. Did I ever tell you about the time I was injected for hay fever and all my fingernails fell out?'

'No.'

'They grew again overnight, luckily. Otherwise I don't know how I should ever have been able to say mass. People talk about the sufferings inflicted by the Gestapo. It's nothing to some of the things I have had to put up with.'

'I'm rather in the dog-house too,' said Norman.

He did not see why Lubbock should always hog all the share of the moment's sufferings.

'Really? But not for long. Look at me. My insides rotting away. These wretched injections. Did I tell you? I've got to have a lot of injections before going away. The last time I was injected was for hay fever and all my fingernails fell out. Then I've got to fly in an aeroplane. I hate flying. It's not that I am frightened of it. Quite the reverse. I was once a fighter pilot in the RAF. But I just hate the sensation. Every time we went out on a night raid my stomach turned to jelly.'

'You told me once that you were at school during the war – a slum school in the East End, wasn't it? And you had to sleep in the tube stations before you were evacuated?'

'Very likely.'

'I've been sent down here for preaching a sermon.'

'When's it going to happen? Don't go on too long, Shotty, will you?'

'I've already preached it.'

'Really? I'm sorry I missed it. I don't always get to Mass these days. Don't know how it is. Something to do with my feet, I think.'

'It was in Westminster Cathedral.'

'Well, it would be. Good old Shotty. You're only asked to preach in the grand places now, of course. The only time I ever preached in Westminster Cathedral – or, rather, was *meant* to preach – I was too ill to manage it. They said it was 'flu, but I'm sure it was paratyphoid. You should have seen the colour of my diarrhoea.'

Norman returned to his perusal of the *Tablet*. Lubbock's egotism was impenetrable; his fantasies more extreme, his 'grip' less strong than ever. He had, in fact, greatly deteriorated since last seen. Norman was glad that he would not have to be putting up with it for much longer.

His own future now seemed as much in doubt as it had done before Christmas. While he paced about the gardens later that morning in the drizzle, he began to wish that he had had the courage of his convictions and left the Institute after his visit to the Gobi Club. It had been a mistake to have been seduced by the glare of publicity. It had brought no pleasure: only hopes which now lay shattered. Now, although he hated everything about it, there seemed even less chance of his being able to leave.

A bell summoned him in to lunch. There were not many priests there, mostly silent men, who had come down to write books or wait for death. The great virtue of the retreat house over the house in Mayfair was that some of the old-fashioned customs still lingered. Most notably, there was no talking at meals. It meant that, for the duration of luncheon and dinner at least, one did not have to listen to catalogues of Lubbock's sufferings and achievements. Instead, one listened to the sufferings and achievements of the Alfonsine saints, which, if no more edifying, at least made a change.

Father O'Shea, the novice master, was reading from the life of the founder, Saint Alfonso of Barcelona.

'So early did the young Alfonso's devotion to Our Lord manifest itself, that from the age of two, he was accustomed to make visits to the church near his home to pray. On one occasion, his nursemaid upbraided him and told him that it was time for him to sleep. But remembering the time when His Lord was lost in the Temple, Alphonso turned on her in a rage and said, "Do you not know that I must worship the Blessed Sacrament day and night?" He prayed to Our Lady for the nursemaid, who was instantly struck dumb, and shortly afterwards died of leprosy . . .

'Throughout his life, Saint Alfonso was subject to acute pain in his feet. "Those who tread the way of Calvary must expect pain," he used to say. And, to show how willingly he accepted his sufferings, he would sometimes plunge his feet into a fire. Miraculously they were never consumed. After his death, his feet were cut off and they are preserved in a special reliquary in Barcelona. Many are the lame men who have walked, after being touched by these most holy relics . . '

It was not exactly calculated to increase one's appetite, but then, neither was the food. Norman munched his way through some Spam as he listened. When the reading was over, Father O'Shea said that, while the lessons contained in the *Life of the Founder* were still of value, the spirit in which it was written was not; and that the magnificent baroque reliquary containing his feet had been destroyed in the recent reforms to make way for a loudspeaker system. This, he emphasized, was all for the good.

In the quiet moments which he managed to snatch away from Lubbock, Norman had time to think. He was not particularly good at thinking, and things only occurred to him long after they should have done. But the injustice of his suspension was beginning to rankle. What had been so wrong with his sermon? It was vulgar, florid, and Victorian. But that was not what Father Cassidy had found so objectionable about it. It had offended a new orthodoxy by echoing an old one. It was alien to the set-up in which Norman now found himself; a set-up which esteemed loudspeaker-systems more highly than the feet of the saints.

Not esteeming either very highly, Norman did not know what to do. The true nature of the Catholic Church was only beginning to dawn on him. He had thought of it as vaguely romantic, exotic, mysterious, beautiful; a power-house of mystery and beauty larger than himself, in which he could find peace and serenity. It *was* a power-house, but not a beautiful one. And he was yet to find a moment's peace, especially while any services were in progress.

In order to escape the Community Mass on Sunday morning, Norman went down to the local Catholic Church for his devotions. The fact that Belief, in a formal sense, was now so elusive, did not weaken his sense that he ought to observe the forms.

The little church looked friendly and inviting in the distance. It had clearly been built in the nineteenth century to make Anglican converts feel at home when they went to Mass. The Pugin spire pointed delicately upwards to a spring sky.

Norman was a little late in arriving, and he had to squeeze in the back row behind a family of six children under the age of eight. They all wriggled and screamed and picked their noses, and made it hard for Norman to follow what was going on.

For some reason, the High Altar, which was visible even

70

from where Norman sat, was not in use. All the chairs in the body of the church had been turned sideways to face a wall, where someone had placed a Scandinavian oak table, decorated with asymmetrically arranged home-made candles. The bread for the Mass was being put into the little wicker baskets now familiar to Norman. They were the sort of thing pubs use for serving scampi and chips. The chalice was of space-age design, made out of stainless steel.

After the Gloria, sung to a jaunty tune, the congregation sang a ghastly song that sounded as if it had been made up by the choir-master on the spur of the moment.

'Thank You for giving me the morning, Thank You for every day that's new,
Thank You that I can know my worries can be cast on You.'

Norman was no poet, but even he flinched at the jollity and lack of scansion.

It was true that he did not have a very religious understanding of things, either. For him, it was all utterly mysterious, and language or liturgy which attempted to explain it in down-to-earth, everyday terms only made it more meaningless, adding to its irrationality a lack of taste. Yet, in the old days, as an Anglican, he had felt glimmerings of faith, or something akin to it, during the Mass. It was because the Mass was incomprehensible and beautiful. The fact that the beauty was stiff, ritualised and remote hinted at things beyond itself, and suggested that through the dark pages of experience, order and light could be glimpsed.

This new Mass, on the contrary, made a cult of ugliness and banality. Its appalling phrases emphasized nothing but the confusion of mind of the people who compiled it. Nothing and No One deserving the name of a God could conceivably be apprehended by it. Perhaps, by its chummy emphasis on good neighbourliness, it might help some nice people to be even nicer. But, as Norman had been taught to understand religion by the few people in the Church of England who appeared to know anything about it, religion was not supposed to make people *nice*. Most people were simply not nice, and it was inane to pretend that they ever could be. Doubtless, the jaunty optimism of the song they were singing was pleasant enough:

'Thank You, O Lord, Your love is boundless.
Thank You that I am full of You.
Thank You, You make me feel so glad and thankful as I do.'

But what if one did not feel full of God? Norman did not, never had done. Nor did he feel glad, or thankful, or loving, or happy. Saint Alfonso of Barcelona, thrusting his bunions into the flames, would, equally, have been unable to join in such a chorus. So would the Psalmist. By implication, it excluded the pinched, unhappy disagreeable majority of the human race and only wanted the *nice* ones. And, as he cast in his mind for a single example of nice behaviour in the New Testament, he could not, at that moment think of one. From the abandoning of Mary and Joseph in the crowds of Jerusalem when the Lord was a child of twelve, to the declaration that one must hate father and mother and kindred for His sake; from the destruction of the Gadarene swine to the withering of the Fig Tree; from the quarrel in the synagogue at Nazareth to the overtuning of the money-changer's tables in the Temple court, it was hard to isolate a single example of chumminess or all friends together. Nor was there much evidence of democracy, or enlightened political views. The early Christians were told to render to Caesar the things that were Caesar's; to be subject to the Emperor Nero, and not to complain about the condition of slavery . . .

So, where did it all come from, this deification of the modern liberal position? As Norman slipped out of the church, before the Mass was over, he realized that he was angry. It was all so ugly and debased. But, worse than that, it was dishonest. Life was not as the song, or the new liturgy, pretended that it was; and nor was the Christian religion. Where was Original Sin; a tainted, fallen, God-created race; a relentless divine justice; only to be appeased by the atonement, an awful grace – where was all this to be fitted in to the new scheme of things? It had simply been thrown out; and Norman began to see why. He did not know, and, at that moment, he did not particularly care, if the Christian religion was true. But he suddenly saw quite clearly that it did not have a hope of winning in the mindless egalitarian world through which he traipsed so drearily. And Father Cassidy and his like were only interested in winning . . .

Father Cassidy, in fact, had driven down from London and wanted to see Norman immediately after luncheon. He seem buoyant and self-confident.

'I hope that you've had time to sort yourself out a bit; do some thinking,' he said aggressively. 'We don't want any Archbishop Lefebvres in England, you know. I can see now with your sentimental Anglican background you probably think a lot of the old fool. You ought to, considering all the money they were paying you. But he's a schismatic. And we want to root his like out of the church.'

'I never really thought about him until you drew my attention to him,' said Norman, anger giving him self-confidence again. 'It is absolutely absurd to think that I was plotting to preach that sermon. If you must know, I got it all out of a book.'

'I suppose you think that makes it better.'

'I don't suppose anything.'

Norman could have punched the Provincial's white, fleshy nose. It was no momentary flash of temper. The tediousness and absurdity of his years in the Institute now appeared in a sinister and dark perspective. He saw Cassidy's energies as an obsession with power. Cold, carefully realized fury was welling up inside him.

'We can't allow any schismatics,' said Father Cassidy coldly.

'And I know why,' said Norman.

'Oh, you do, do you?'

73

'Yes.'

'Why?'

'Because you only want to be on the side that's winning,' said Norman coldly. 'It doesn't matter how often you change the party line, so long as you can accommodate yourself to the mood of the moment. It doesn't matter what's true. It doesn't matter that what you say now contradicts what the Chruch said twenty years ago. You are interested in power, and you know how to ridicule anyone who points out to you the truth. The only voices of protest that the press allows to be heard against all the nonsense that has gone on since the Second Vatican Council are made out to be extreme right-wing crackpots and reactionaries. It's been a perfectly managed job. But I'm bored stiff with the whole thing. All the other Christian denominations have been left high and dry by the twentieth century – and perhaps that's a good place to be. But Rome has had to contort itself into a position that makes it seem that, far from resisting the times, the Church has been calling the tune.'

'This is sad, romantic stuff,' said Cassidy.

'It also happens to be true.'

'Romantics always get bees in their bonnets, and start talking about the truth,' said the priest. 'You'll have time to think about it on the aeroplane. You're leaving London airport tonight.'

'Oh no I'm not.'

Norman was completely taken aback. He had not expected Cassidy to pull this card.

'It's time I told you,' he said. 'I'm leaving the Institute. I tried to tell you before Christmas and you wouldn't let me. I wish I had never been mixed up in it all . . . '

'There's no point in arguing. You fly tonight. The lay brothers here have strict instructions not to let you out of their sight. The doctor is going to give you your injections. It's rather short notice, but it will have to do. I've given Father Lubbock your papers, including a certificate to prove that you had them all done three weeks ago.'

'Lubbock?'

'He'll be going with you. He is a sick man, but he is better now. We'll see how the Peruvian Indians like your beloved Tridentine Mass. My belief is that they won't be very interested in it.'

There was no time to reply to this horrific news. Cassidy was laughing quietly to himself as he left the room. Later that day, he wrote in his notebook: *My original suspicions have proved false. He is plainly not the bumbling reactionary that we thought at first. He is very dangerous. Time will tell, but it looks as if we shall be having more to do with this customer. But can Lubbock be relied on?*

Lubbock was in a low mood in the taxi, and said little. From time to time, he let out miserable little grunts, and his lips were rarely still. Norman could not make out what he was saying, but a gentle burbling continued most of the way into London. Norman was not feeling particularly well himself after the injections. He had had tetanus, typhoid, cholera, rabies, influenza and sleeping sickness all within the space of a few minutes, and he could not believe they had done any good to his system. Perhaps its only consoling feature was that the mingled drugs and diseases in his bloodstream did something to numb the agony of knowing that he was doomed to be stuck in some plague-ridden Peruvian settlement, interfering in the lives of the natives, Lubbock the only English-speaker for miles around.

Lubbock of all people. Norman tried not to look at his companion, but every time he heard one of the burbling noises he could cheerfully have committed murder. Lubbock was to blame for it all, somehow.

The last of England flashed by in the afternoon haze. Semi-detached half-timbered houses of the nineteen-thirties, foot-ball pitches, church spires and pylons caught the eye. Norman felt overpoweringly in love with it all; part of it; in no mood to be separated from it. What right had Cassidy and the rest to be shipping him off, merely because he read a sermon out of a book? He felt weak, impotent, unable to do anything about it.

Norman had thought, in a juvenile way, that most people were pretty awful, until he joined the Church of Rome. He now saw that he was wrong. He didn't know the meaning of the word awful until he had surrounded himself with papists. Some of them were perhaps amiable enough: Freddie Toogood, for instance, was obviously kind and good. But, Cassidy. Lubbock. That insufferable Father Sporran and his repugnant dancing nuns. And to think that he was flying off, in a few hours, to a subcontinent which was full of the people. It was more than flesh and blood could stand.

He tried to console himself with prayer, but it was no good. Belief eluded him, and his words were empty echoes which went nowehere and meant nothing. Then he tried remembering snatches of poetry or Scripture which had helped him in the past.

The only poem that he could remember the whole of was *Excelsior*, and did not seem very appropriate on this occasion. Most of the snatches of Scripture he remembered were sentences of the sort which might be read at the beginning of Anglican evensongs. 'Enter not into judgement with thy servant, O Lord, for in Thy sight shall no man living be justified . . . I will arise and go unto my Father, and will say unto Him . . .'

His father. Why had he not thought of it before? The Colonel would scarcely have had time to leave the Martello tower yet. He had only been there four weeks. But how could he be reached? How could he escape? Lubbock had nearly all the money. Norman himself had no more than a few pounds on his person.

Lubbock was still talking to himself as the car pulled into the air terminal at Cromwell Road. When the car finally stopped, his spirits seemed to brighten.

'Stage One, Shotty old thing,' he said, in his jolly voice. 'Tomorrow to fresh woods and pastures new, eh?'

'Yes,' said Norman.

'Checking in', with Lubbock in charge, was much more complicated than it need have been. They kept finding themselves queueing up at desks meant for passengers from

Ireland, or which only distributed brochures about chartered flights to Turkey. But, eventually, it was done. They were told that their bus would be leaving for the airport in an hour.

'We needn't have got here so early,' said Lubbock. 'How about a little drink while we wait?'

'All right,' said Norman.

'Have you got any money?'

'No. You are meant to have it all.'

'There's something the matter, isn't there?'

'Why do you say that?'

'Well, you are so snappy.'

'I'm not snappy. I just happen to be rather fed up.'

'There's nothing I've done?'

'Nothing specifically.'

'Let's get to the bottom of this.'

Norman sighed. He could not bear Lubbock's brotherly love act.

'I don't much want to go. That's all,' he said.

'Don't want to go? But think of all the experience we shall have together. Someone said to me in the retreat house when they knew that I was going that I had been put out to grass. I gave them a piece of my mind. In my view, this is one of the first sensible things the Provincial has done for a long time. He realizes that what the church needs in South America is not just missionary zeal. They need the chaps with some brains. People like you and me, Shotty. I'm very glad we had that whiff of the charismatic movement before we went. I think that should stand us both in very good stead.'

'How about that drink?'

'Where do you think we get it?'

'In the bar?'

'Let's go and find out.'

'You go and get the drinks, and I'll look after the luggage,' said Norman.

'But we've given the luggage to those Negroes over there on the conveyor belt.'

'Not our hand-luggage.'

'Can't you bring it with you?'

77

'The bar might be crowded.'

'Just as you like,' said Lubbock. 'Look after my camera for me, will you? It's not insured, and it cost a couple of hundred.'

Norman knew perfectly well that this was untrue. But now was no time to be devoting to Lubbock's mendacity. There might not be another opportunity before they reached the airport. Picking up his hold-all, he got up and walked across the crowded 'foyer'. His heart beat furiously. He looked about him furtively. He felt that everyone was watching him; that crowd of West German businessmen; the Arabs heaving crocodile-skin suitcases on to conveyor belts; the air-hostesses who walked briskly about, smiling at everyone. Just as he got to the big glass doors, he stopped in his tracks. There was a clergyman staring him full in the face.

He felt all the irrational fear which a criminal would have, meeting a policeman just outside the house where he had committed a burglary. The clergyman looked at him quizzically.

'Have we met before?'

'I . . .'

'Pitter, isn't it?'

'No. My name is Shotover.'

'Thank God,' said the clergyman. 'I had a curate called Pitter once who went mad and jumped off the pier at Margate. I've always been afraid that he would come back to haunt me. I see him all over the place. You look a bit like him.'

'Thank you,' said Norman, rushing past him so fast that it was as if he vanished into air.

The clergyman stared after him in puzzlement.

'I'm sure it was Pitter,' he murmured.

Outside, Norman ran. He did not care which direction he went in, so long as he got there fast.

People were coming out of work. He dived on and off the pavement to avoid them, running through the dusk to Earl's Court, and not stopping until he plunged into the safety of the Underground station. Meeting the clergyman had upset him badly; knocked him off balance. Was he mad? Or was it some trick of Cassidy's?

Rush hour had reached its height before he boarded his train. He felt only half-safe mingling in the crowds. Every other face looked like Cassidy.

But, when he had caught an Upminster train and stood, sandwiched in among dozens of anonymous faces, all swaying to and fro like clothes on a coat-hanger, he smiled grimly at his own daring. It was only the word TOWER at Tower Hill station which shook him out of his smug reverie. He got out of the train and began to wonder what to do next.

When Lubbock saw that his own plan had worked, he drank down Norman's whisky, and went to the reception desk to cash in the tickets. Then he caught a taxi for Hampstead Heath.

Locating Colonel Shotover was not always easy, given the almost Bedouin existence he chose to live, moving house at least every six months, and spending most of that time looking for 'something a bit more suitable'. Norman rarely knew where he was and, had he not received notice of the fact on the back of his Christmas card, he would not know now.

The Martello Tower, near Wimbridge on Sea.

Wimbridge was accessible by the railway. Norman had just enough money to get there, and, had he not tried to save it by hitch-hiking and found himself being driven to Weybridge, he would have been there sooner than the next afternoon.

It was a dingy little resort, which had not been there until someone in the eighteen-eighties had thought how suitably dull it would be were nannies to take children to it for the ozone.

It was some time, having explored streets full of houses with names like DUNROMIN and THE ANCHORAGE, that Norman was directed to the cliffs.

To describe the Martello Tower as 'near' Wimbridge on Sea had been a piece of fancy on the part of the Post Office which Norman came to resent, as he trudged his way along the footpath on top of the cliffs, with the sea-mists and the shadows of early evening beginning to envelop him. He must have walked about a mile before the tower came into sight.

It was entirely the sort of place he would have expected his father to favour: inaccessible by any but the roughest road vehicle; impractical for anything which most people would think of as the considerations of everyday life; impressive, romantic, impossible.

He could see it quite clearly, lit up on the horizon. He could almost make out the pattern of the curtains in the windows. And yet, the longer he walked, the more the tower seemed to shrink away in the distance. Dark had actually fallen, and the sea-mists had turned to fog, as Norman turned in at the gate.

The small garden by the front door had been neglected on an almost Gothic scale. Knee-high grass, uncut during the previous summer, choked the divisions between lawn and flower-beds. But, inside, there were lights on, and the wireless was blaring out a news bulletin.

There was no reply when he knocked on the door, but he attributed this to his father's increasing deafness. He knocked again; and, again receiving no answer, he turned the handle. The door was open, and he stepped inside.

'Hallo!'

The word echoed round the empty hall. There was the familiar hat-stand, with four dusty old bowlers, echoes of the Colonel's former career in 'business', any quantity of umbrellas and a few cloth caps. On the wall beside it was the looking-glass, and the painting of the battle of Trafalgar. He suddenly wondered if his father was all right.

The wireless still blared out its flow of information about the troubled doings of the world. Then the news stopped, and the weather forecast spoke of imminent storms over the Channel. Probably the old man was asleep. Norman stepped inside.

It was a large, rather beautiful room, part studio, part drawing-room, with a great window looking towards the sea.

His father was not there, but almost every object spoke of his presence: the half-finished canvases, mostly landscapes in the post-impressionist manner; the framed photographs of himself; the sherry bottles, and the newspapers. Familiar objects of furniture caught Norman's eye. In the window stood the magnificent Bechstein grand, never played, in Norman's recollection, since the death of an uncle in 1959; the glass-fronted bureau, made in the reign of George II, and looking as if someone had been stuffing it with bundles of letters ever since; the handsome Chesterfield, upholstered in red velvet, faded by years of sunlight; the writing-table, piled with water-colours, sketch-books and correspondence. Norman picked up one letter. It was dated 1961. Underneath it were some of his old school reports.

It is a pity that he has not carried on with the oboe . . . What his former-master has written about his Greek grammar could very well be applied to all areas of his life in the school. He has yet to learn that what one gets out *of a school such as this is very much dependent on what one is prepared to put* in . . .

All his life, people had been making demands of this sort which he felt unable to live up to. Now he was thirty, and he still had not 'improved'. He knew that he was meant to be *doing* something, and, as far as he could make out, it did not really matter what. But people were dissatisfied unless one could present some front to the world which could be seen as acceptable activity. Merely 'drifting' – one of his house-master's favourite words – as his father did, would not do.

He was just beginning to become seriously worried about his father, when his eye drifted to the chimney-piece, where a large piece of white card, decorated in the Colonel's distinctive, florid calligraphy, read: GONE TO SCOTLAND.

This was just Norman's luck. And it was typical of his father to go away leaving the front door open and the wireless on. The old man had a horror of being locked out of his own home – wherever that happened to be – and he never carried a key for fear of losing it.

Norman decided to go upstairs and explore the rest of the tower. Even if he failed to see his father, he could at least stay the night here. It was safe. Cassidy and the others would be unlikely to follow him down here. It was the first time in his life that he felt his father's inaccessible and anti-social mode of existence had something to be said for it.

There appeared to be two rooms upstairs, and a sort of attic solid with junk. One of the rooms was evidently his father's bedroom. Apart from the furniture, which was unfamiliar to him, it gave off the same smells as all his bedrooms did, wherever he made his transitory stays. A mixture of bay-rum and boot polish.

It would be misleading to describe the other room as a spare bedroom, since that would be to suggest that the Colonel ever expected visitors. But there was a bed in it, and a great deal of other furniture not wanted in other regions of the tower. Norman put one of his suitcases down on a chair, and drew the bed covers. There were a few army blankets folded up on the bed. They would do. He decided not to bother with sheets.

As he turned to descend the staircase once more, intending to forage in the kitchen, if there was one, he heard a lavatory flushing.

He started, as if he had heard a ghost. He had so much adapted to the idea that he was alone in the tower that the gurgling cistern seemed positively spectral. A door opened in the shadows half-way up the stairs and a figure came clumping down towards him. For a nightmarish moment, it looked just like Father Cassidy.

'Squitters,' it said. 'It's all this damned fluoride stuff they put in the water round here.'

'Dad. I thought that you were in Scotland.'

'Wish I was. Well, I will be, as a matter of fact, as soon as I can get the estate agents round here to sell this place. By rights it ought to be levelled to the ground.'

'I've just got here.'

This seemed a superfluous observation in the circumstances, but he did not know what to say. Conversation never flowed between them easily.

'Don't drink the water, whatever you do. I haven't touched a drop since I arrived. Just rinse my teeth in the stuff at nights, and that's enough to knock me out.'

'I thought I'd come down and look you up.'

They descended the stairs together and walked into the studio, where they yelled at one another over the voices of the Archers.

'Did you get that school-teaching job?'

'I wasn't looking for a school-teaching job.'

'Thought you were.'

'I've decided to leave the order.'

'The doctors round here want shooting. I've tried to get hold of three of them to give me some Kaolin Morphine. They don't even answer the bloody telephone.'

'I'm sorry that you aren't well.'

'I'm all right. Are you listening to this tripe, or shall I switch it off?'

'Switch it off.'

'Can't stand that Walter Gabriel,' said the Colonel. Not having adjusted to the prevailing silence, he was still shouting at the top of his voice. 'I'm only sorry you can't stay,' he added.

'I thought I would.'

'There's no room,' said the Colonel. 'No room at all.'

'What about that room on the landing?'

'I'm still sorting things out in there.'

'It looked all right to me.'

'I wouldn't put a dog to sleep in there. Too much junk. You accumulate a lot of junk over the years.' He gestured towards the untidy room. 'Every time I move, I think I'll sort it out. Then I don't get round to it.'

'Perhaps you'd like some help.'

'Very kind of you, but I'm better on my own. Besides, you'll want to be getting back to school.'

'But I left school years ago.'

'Did you? Didn't think you'd tried it yet. Needs a bit of getting used to, the discipline. Your Uncle Roderick did it for a time, you know. Taught at Rugby. Then he got the sack. Usual trouble, I'm afraid.'

'I didn't know.'

'Oh, yes. Still, that won't affect you. You'll love it. If I were you, I should write off at once to the Headmaster. I'm afraid I can't have you about much longer. There are workmen coming. And, besides, I shall be away; out of this place as soon as I can fix up the croft . . . '

Norman wondered if his father had gone mad. Then he looked down at the Personal Column of *The Times* which the Colonel was holding out to him. If the Colonel said he could not stay, he could not stay. And, besides, what would he do for money? He needed a job at once, and perhaps a school was not such a bad idea. One of the entries had been ringed with purple ink.

Wanted immediately, he read. *English master, due to sudden retirement, at private school in North London. Previous experience preferred. Own salary scale. Accommodation available. Apply, in writing, to the Headmaster, Peacham House, Near Pinner, as soon as possible.*

5

LEAD, KINDLY LIGHT

'Now, in this scene, Banquo starts to smell a rat . . . '

'Pooh! What a stink!'

'Who said that?'

'Said that, sir? I didn't say *that*, sir.'

'It was you, sir. You said *rat*, sir.'

'Don't be silly, Macracken.'

'I wasn't, sir. You said Banquo was smelly, and I said . . . '

'That's quite enough. The next person to talk will have to write out three hundred lines. Now. That's better. In this scene, as I said –'

'It was you, sir! You were the next person to talk. You'll have to do three hundred lines. Naughty sir!'

'Macracken, I shan't warn you again. Banquo begins to suspect that Macbeth has murdered Duncan. We shall all have the same parts as last time.'

'Sir, that's unfair. You never let me read.'

'That's because you don't read properly, Davis.'

'He reads better than Hassif, sir. Hassif can't read at all.'

'Be quiet. It's very good practice for Hassif. Come on, Hassif – Thou hast it now: King, Cawdor, Glamis, all. As the weird women promised . . . '

'Ooh! Weird!'

'Macracken! That is your last chance. The next time, it will be three hundred lines.'

'*Zoo harst eet naking. Cow-door Clarmees . . . *'

'Sir, he's lousy; he can't read; let me read, sir. Please, sir, I promise, I'll do it properly, sir. Honestly, sir.'

'All right, Davis. Perhaps, after all, it is a bit difficult for Hassif to read the part of Banquo. Follow it in your book, Hassif, while Davis reads. Now, Davis. Remember that Macbeth is a friend of yours, and , as well as being jealous of his success, you are sorry that you don't think he's been playing fair.'

'Right ho, sir. Thou has it. Now, King Cawdor, Glamis all. As the weird women promised and I fear. Thou play'd most foully for't . . . '

'What's for't, sir?'

'A Scotch castle, you twit.'

'Macracken. I really shan't warn you again.'

Norman sat back at his desk as the scene got under way. He was glad that he had turned out to be such a success as a teacher. There was nothing to it, once one had the discipline under control. There was only one class who really frightened him, and he did not have to teach them for more than three lessons a week.

It had all been absurdly easy. Twelve months had passed since he ran away from Lubbock at the air terminal, and no one from the Institute had written so much as a letter to find out where he was or what he was doing. Child's play. He had originally thought that he ought to get away from London, and look for some school in Northumberland or Cornwall; change his name; invent a past for himself. But he had decided it was unnecessary, and two terms had proved him right. It was nice being in the suburbs. When school became tedious or depressing, all he had to do was to get on a train, and within half an hour he was at Baker Street. His colleagues never asked about his past. The Headmaster, at the interview, had seemed only vaguely interested in the fact that he had been a Catholic priest; the only really urgent question, it seemed, was whether he was prepared to supervise the annual Scout camp. Most other masters seemed to know nothing about him. Perhaps they either assumed that he had arrived fresh from the University, or that he had come on from some other teaching job.

The life had many pleasures. He became an enthusiastic scoutmaster. He even enjoyed refereeing the hockey; and several people had commented on how well he had produced *Julius Caesar* as Junior School play in the previous term. The money was not particularly good, but it was better than nothing, which was what he had been used to. There was always a certain amount in his current account at the end of each month. No one bothered him. He was relaxed; detached; in a sober way, happy.

Above all, he felt the pleasure, new every morning, of not being a Catholic priest. It was months since he had heard the word *charismatic*; months since he had heard mass; he knew no nuns and he heard no confessions. It had almost been worth the three time-wasting years with the Institute to feel the sense of peace and liberation.

Technically speaking, of course, he was still a Catholic priest. He had not gone through any ceremony to deprive him of his orders. He had not seen the point of doing so. He had no immediate intention of getting married. Most of the house-masters' daughters were fairly goofy. He had looked up his status in a book. At the moment, according to the rules of the Institute, he was a *fugitivus* or runaway. There seemed a kind of appropriateness in that. Cassidy and the rest would never find him now. If they did, he would move on. Nothing would persuade him to go back, and no amount of threatening would work either.

'We hear our bloody cousins are bestowed
In England and in Ireland, not confessing . . . '
'Sir, isn't that swearing, sir?'
'No, Macracken.'
'If I said that my bloody cousins were in Ireland, it would be swearing, wouldn't it, sir?'
'Yes.'
'Well, then, why isn't it when Shakespeare says it, sir?'

He was saved by the bell. As soon as the lesson ended, all the boys tore out of the class-room, anxious not to miss a second of their luncheon-hour. There were cries of 'Wait for me!' and 'Save a place for me in the queue!'

It had been a five-period morning, always tiring. Norman gathered up the books on his desk. He had forgotten to set their prep. Never mind. All the less marking to do at the end of the week. Although the term was only ten days old, an awful lot of exercise books had accumulated in his room already.

He looked up to see the dark, mournful eyes of Hassif staring plaintively at him.

'Sir, you no like my book.'
'Your book?'
'Sir no like book.'
'Don't be silly, old boy.'
'No like. Me read. Me read no very good?'
'Oh, that. I thought you read very well, Hassif. With a bit more practice, it will be impossible to tell you apart from the English boys. Have you been practising your conversational English?'
'Sir?'

87

'You learn speak? You speak English?'

'I speak very good, yes.'

'Who teaches you?'

'Mahomet. He teach. Very good.'

In spite of all the effort people made to split the Hassif twins up and make them speak properly, they were still inseparable. Norman found them rather a bore, but, as junior English master, he was responsible for making sure that they had three or four hours' practice conversation each week. He was paid extra for it, but he resented the time it took up. He felt that the same trouble would not be taken for other boys. The Headmaster kept emphasizing that the Hassifs should not be given preferential treatment, and that they were to be treated like everyone else. But he plainly did not practise what he preached. There was going to be a new language laboratory called the Hassif Block. The boys themselves lived in the Headmaster's house in a bedroom which was kept locked at nights.

No one was supposed to know who the twins were, but it was common knowledge that their father was a big oil magnate in the Middle East. An Embassy car arrived for them every Saturday afternoon after games, and delivered them again before Chapel on Monday mornings.

'We come to you this afternoon, very good?'

'Very good, Hassif.'

'You no like reading. I no read good?'

The child looked wounded, distraught.

'You read very good.'

Norman sauntered off down the corridor, throwing his gown over his shoulder. He felt in need of his lunch.

He had come to love the ugly Victorian school buildings. Before he took up the job, he thought that an ideal school, for his purposes, should have two qualities: it should be sufficiently large to enable him to be anonymous, and it should be Protestant. Peacham House was both. Founded in the last century for the education of sons of evangelical clergymen, it sprawled for acre upon valuable acre within easy distance of the Metropolitan line. There were about five hundred boys, all of them boarders, except the fifty or so who came in by train each day from Watford, Harrow or Dollis Hill. None of their fathers, so far as Norman knew, were evangelical clergymen. The Hassifs, at any rate, were Moslems, and that was even better, from his point of view.

He ambled down the lugubrious, neo-Gothic corridors until he reached the common-room, where he flung his gown over the back of a chair. Schoolmasters huddled about it in small groups, smoking pipes, reading the newspapers, or perfecting their imitations of the Headmaster, Mr Sale. In fact, Sale defied parody. And it was presumably the elusive, low-key quality of his dreadfulness which kept the imitators so busy. Norman went up to the notice-boards to see if there had been anything new put up since the eleven o'clock Recess.

Several typed notices from Sale had appeared. *The attention of colleagues is drawn to the fact that boys are not standing in straight lines in the lunch queue* . . . one began. And another pointed out that litter was accumulating near the Scout huts.

'Seen the news?' said a jolly voice beside Norman. It was Johnson, the German master, the closest thing that he had to a friend on the staff. Mrs Johnson was a pretty woman who gave Norman supper on Sunday evenings, and Johnson kept him amused with a perpetual flow of anecdotes about the absurdity and grotesque behaviour of his other colleagues.

'What news?'

'They've found a replacement for poor old Bottoms.'

'At this stage of the term?'

'No one knows who he is, but Sale has been boasting to everyone that he is a doctor of philosophy. I don't know what use that will be when teaching Latin to the fifth form, but still.'

The departure of their colleague Mr Bottoms, shortly before the end of the previous term, had been one of the more exciting events since Norman's arrival in the school. The boys had ragged the man unmercifully, and it had had a bad effect on his nerves. Several stories were already going round, most of them originating with Johnson, about the final fate of Bottoms. They ranged from his having been locked away in a mental asylum to his having left for Morocco and a change of sex. His departure, on the whole, was a relief to his colleagues. They saw what the boys meant. He had been stubborn. Anyone else would have seen the force of their advice to stop using the after-shave lotion, said to be the source of his discipline problems. Others said that the affair was much more complicated than it seemed, and that a major quarrel had developed with Sale. This was quite likely. Indeed, quarrels with Sale were hard to avoid, given the highly idiosyncratic way in which he chose to run the school.

'He's arriving tonight,' Johnson said. 'So you'll see him at your residents' supper.'

Their voices were drowned by roars of laughter at the opposite corner of the room. Someone, it seemed, had at last managed to catch Sale's accent to perfection.

'That's quite enough, gentlemen,' this genius said. 'Now, perhaps one of you ought to be making sure the lunch-queue isn't running riot.'

This was too much for them. Pipes had to be put down, beer abandoned, to give vent to full-scale belly-laughs. Then, the noise stopped almost at once. The room began to empty. Johnson was nowhere to be seen. Over by the pigeon holes, Norman caught sight of Sale, crimson with embarrassment and annoyance.

'Ah,' he said, 'Mr Shotover.'

'Good morning, Headmaster.'

Sale had this way of creeping up on one unawares. It was partly that he was so small. One never saw him until it was too late. Some of the history masters said that Napoleon had benefited from the same tactical advantages over his fellows.

'It's about the Hassif twins,' said Sale.

'I was meaning to ask you about them myself, sir. I was wondering if it would not be possible for someone else to teach them this term, sir.'

'Someone else?'

'It has been rather a strain. They hardly know any English at all.'

90

'But you are meant to be teaching it to them. It's hardly their fault if they don't know it.'

'But they speak to each other all the time in Arabic.'

'Then stop them. I must make a note of that,' Sale added, jotting something down in a notebook. 'Thank you for telling me. But I am afraid that there is no possiblity of any other colleague taking over the Hassifs just yet. We must all pull our weight, Mr Shotover. This is what a school like this stands for.'

'Yes, sir.'

Sale drew himself up to his full four foot eleven and paced off, his gown rustling with self-importance. He had a lot to do that afternoon, including seeing three prospective parents, and telling the Bursar to get a room ready for the new master.

Supper for the resident bachelors was not the jolliest aspect of life at Peacham House. The brighter sparks were either married, or took care to live a healthy distance away from the school. It meant that only those too mean or too idle to seek alternative accommodation were left to share supper together in the evenings. Norman often felt that readings from the life of St Alfonso of Barcelona would have been preferable to the morose and desultory attempts at conversation which characterized that table.

Musgrove sat at the end. He was a pompous, red-faced young man who had a way of beaming down the table at the rest of his colleagues in amusement at his own remarks, as if trying to summon up the atmosphere of some cosy, rather minor Oxford college. In terms of his own fantasy life, this was doubtless where Musgrove believed himself to be.

Quirk was there, too, growing fatter each day, his little piggy eyes staring about him with glints of impenetrable sadism.

Musgrove and Quirk were usually the only masters to speak at meals. They did not speak to each other. It was more that they pursued rival monologues which the rest of the company sat through in silence.

'Shall we wait for our new colleague, or shall we begin?'

asked Musgrove, in his characteristically fruity tones.

Quirk, less in reply than as an observation of his own, said, 'If he doesn't come soon, the soup will be cold.'

This was a fairly safe prediction. In the year that Norman had spent eating meals in that room, the soup had never been anything else. Tonight, of all nights, one resented the fact. It was February at its most bitter.

This talk of their new colleague directed all eyes to the empty chair on Musgrove's left.

'I wonder where old Bottoms is now,' someone said.

There was a general snigger.

'Our good headmaster has come up with a PhD, forsooth,' Musgrove pontificated. 'An American, I fancy. He seems to have a degree from some establishment in the mid-west.'

Having been to a fairly insignificant provincial university himself, Musgrove was always anxious to belittle the academic background of everyone else.

'A sallow youth, I shouldn't wonder,' he continued. 'Vegetarian, perhaps. A draft-dodger, or some such. In sandals, I shouldn't wonder. Still, we must be tolerant, dear colleagues, and take what comes.'

'If he is a vegetarian,' said Quirk, in a rare concession to having noticed a remark made by anyone but himself, 'he won't want any of that ox-tail soup.'

'Two minutes, Quirk, old boy; two minutes.'

Musgrove stirred the noxious brown fluid in the tureen and sniffed disconsolately.

Quirk's eyes were almost popping through his absurd, Billy-Bunterish spectacles. He was, Norman thought, most certainly more obese than the night before; just as gnomic; just as insanely appreciative of some private joke he was having at the rest of the world's expense.

No level of ingenious speculation could plumb what fantasies *he* inhabited. His only interests in life appeared to be railways and eating. He was immensely knowledgeable about the first subject. He had even composed several monographs (often hinting that they were to be published) on such topics as 'Coupling in Yugoslavia' and 'Sleepers in the

Environs of Crewe'. His passion for food was less specialized, and he was in no sense a gourmand. He never went to restaurants; he was much too mean. He simply liked stuffing himself with whatever happened to be available, and could be found in the dining-room where they now sat at most hours of the day, making sandwiches, raiding the biscuit tin, and drinking endless glasses of milk.

'Perhaps we shouldn't wait,' said Musgrove.

'Transatlantic travel evidently takes longer than anticipated,' said Quirk, adjusting his napkin, and beaming at his choice of words. As with everything he said, there was no possibility of reply; nor was there meant to be. Everyone looked embarrassed. It was the conversational equivalent of his teaching methods; he was said to be able to reduce the boys to tears faster than any other man on the staff.

'Two minutes are up,' he added. 'Two minutes and forty-one seconds, to be precise.'

Obviously, the habitual perusal of railway timetables had made him used to thinking in such extraordinary units of time.

'Well, good Doctor,' said Musgrove, 'I fear that we shall start without you.'

And, with this rhetorical flourish, he started dishing out the soup.

Like most things Musgrove said, it turned out to be wrong. The words had not left his lips before the window flew open, and a pair of very dirty gloves, suggestive of a sort used by burglars in the Sherlock Holmes stories, grabbed the orange curtains from the outside and drew them apart. Swirls of almost ludicrously theatrical fog, again reminiscent of the works of Conan Doyle, puffed into the room from the darkness without, and an angry voice called out, 'Is every bloody door in this place locked?'

Everyone turned to stare at the dark rectangle between the swaying curtains, wondering what would intrude.

A Gladstone bag, keeping up the motive of late nineteenth-century fiction, flew into the room first, springing open just beside Musgrove's chair to reveal any quantity of books and some underwear in a sensationally filthy condition.

'My dear fellow,' said Musgrove, leaving the table. 'Wait one moment, and I can open a door for you.'

But a boot, dripping with mud, had been hoisted on to the window ledge. Beyond it could be seen a scaly, white, hairless leg; no traces of a sock; a little further up, hints of a trouser made from mole-catcher's cord. A shoulder in bright russet tweed then presented itself, and, after a good deal of cursing and swearing, they saw a man's back view, brushing himself down, and drawing the curtains once more.

'Easily done,' he said. 'Not that it can have done much good to my hernia.'

He held out a hand, scarcely cleaner than the glove which had encased it, to Musgrove.

Lubbock's appearance had changed since Norman had last seen him, wandering off in the direction of the bar at the Cromwell Road air terminal. He looked more cheerful, more self-confident, but it was hard to say that he looked better. Growing a beard had not helped. It was a scrubby thing, infesting the lower regions of a much emaciated face in uneven clumps, and emphasizing how unhealthy the complexion had become. He was very blotchy. Drink, not the open air, was responsible for the touches of redness. Orange teeth, fewer than there had been twelve months before, grinned between the gaps in a pathetically cheerful mouth. It was a while before Norman recognized him.

Lubbock himself showed no awareness that there was anyone in the room who might have known him in earlier stages of life.

'Smith is the name,' he said. 'Unusual name, but there it is. The family name is Myth, but my grandfather changed it.'

The fact that he was very drunk only became apparent at a fairly late stage of the meal. After a certain amount of stuffing underpants back into the Gladstone bag, removal of his tie, acceptance of Musgrove's offer of a second glass of sherry, Lubbock was prevailed upon to sit down and eat his soup.

He took his place next to Norman, winked heavily, and then slurped into the ox-tail for a while. Then he gestured towards the Gladstone bag and spoke to Musgrove.

'It was difficult to know what to bring.'

His eyes never left his luggage for more than an instant, as if someone was going to steal it, insist on searching its contents, throw it back out of the window.

'The car broke down just outside Hendon of all places. I left my trunk there. That lot should get me through the first week's teaching.'

'My dear chap,' said Musgrove. 'Engine trouble?'

Quirk began an analysis of the various possiblities offered to the railway passenger trying to find his way from Hendon. He indicated the infrequency of trains from mainline stations after the subsidence of the rush-hour, weighing them against the frequent changes necessary if it were decided to pick a way on the Bakerloo line.

Lubbock stared at him in incomprehension.

'I don't know what you are talking about,' he said.

'Perhaps my speculations have been a trifle complex.'

Quirk beamed at the notion. Although piqued at having been deprived of a second helping of soup, and hungry in anticipation of the gammon to follow, the extraction of such an admission from a new colleague at such an early stage of the game was a prize not to be disdained.

'You probably made the mistake of catching a stopping-train after you go to Wembley,' he added. 'The thing to do, assuming that you did pass through Wembley, is to change and catch one on the Metropolitan line. They only stop at Harrow-on-the-Hill. Otherwise you find yourself stopping at Neasden, Dollis Hill – '

'Christ in heaven, man! If you think I had allowed myself to be caught up on the railways, should I be here now?'

Norman groaned inwardly. He could feel the peaceful little world that he had carved out for himself over the last twelve months being shattered by every breath that Lubbock took, every word that he spoke. Now that his enjoyment of it was over, he could see what he had liked about the school. It was all so delightfully low-key. Musgrove and Quirk might be tiresome. The Headmaster even more so. But they did not expect life to be lived on the operatically emotional pitch which suited Lubbock, and the world from which Norman believed himself to have escaped. Nor did their intrigues and quarrels match up to the alarmingly sinister scale of Father Cassidy's exercise of personal power.

'The school *is* very difficult to find,' Musgrove was saying. It was the usual opening to his story of the Master of Balliol getting lost one evening on his way to address the Historical Society.

'It was easy enough,' Lubbock laughed.

'How *did* you come?' Norman asked.

The topic itself was not particularly interesting, but he felt several reasons for wanting to talk. First, it seemed unnatural not to speak to a man whom he had known, on and off, for the last four years. Secondly, anything to stop Musgrove talking. Thirdly, most important of all, he felt seduced once more by the peculiar magic exuded by Lubbock, as by most egotists, which made it appear desireable to discuss the most trivial of his personal arrangements.

He looked at Norman with the same, rather guilty, dog-like smile, winked again, and grunted. Since most of the faces round that table were fairly extraordinary, Lubbock's inane expression did not seem very conspicuous. Lubbock's smile should have been a warning signal; but it wasn't. Norman took no notice. In fact, it represented a very heavy stage of inebriation. He grunted again, as if Norman had made a joke which he did not find particularly funny.

Then he held a sherry-glass to his lips, allowing the last drop which remained at the bottom to trickle down into his mouth.

Quirk rang for the gammon and pineapple chunks, leathery at the best of times, and which did not look as if they had improved by keeping.

Musgrove began some rather ponderous speculations about the meat's age, pretending to recognize individual slices, as he doled them out on to the plates, as ones rejected from meals taken during the previous week. Someone else, for once, was talking too; something about the First Eleven's prospects in next month's hockey against Merchant Taylors', Harrow and Haberdasher's Aske.

Lubbock suddenly tapped the table with his fork, as if calling for silence.

'If no one minds,' he declaimed angrily, 'I was just about to answer my friend here's question about how I made my way this evening from Hendon.'

'Steady on,' Norman muttered.

'Hendon,' repeated Lubbock. He contemplated the place-name for a moment dramatically, as if its resonances should call up associations of poetry and magnificence: like Carthage, Ithaca, or Fontarabbia. Then, with a broad, dramatic gesture which upset the water-jug, he said, 'What do they know of Hendon, who only Hendon know?'

There was water everywhere, dripping from the edge of the table on to Norman's trousers, splashing into the salt, soaking up the paper napkins which had been placed in a pile near the artificial flowers at the centre of the table.

Quirk, always pleased by a calamity, began to waddle about the room looking for a cloth, and assuring Lubbock, in a manner calculated to be as disconcerting as possible, that there was nothing to worry about.

Lubbock, for his part, did not appear to notice Quirk's implied courtesy. If he even saw what had happened to the water, most of which poured over Norman, he did not show any signs of it, but launched into a narrative of fantastic improbability which culminated in his having walked the twelve or so miles from Hendon.

'It is perfectly easy once you have located the pole star,' he kept saying, waving his empty sherry-glass, and leaving piles of uneaten chips on his plate to grow cold. 'Not bad, this stuff,' he added. 'I could take more of it, if offered.'

Partly out of a desire to see what would happen, partly out of malice, Norman got up and began to fill his glass. Musgrove and Quirk began to exchange looks of a conspiratorial nature. Clearly, the immediate problem, from their point of view, was how to dispose of him before he passed out, made a scene, or was actually sick, in the presence of the

Headmaster, who usually came to take coffee in the evenings with the bachelors.

Both of them were fairly shameless in their obsequiousness to Sale, and it was no secret that they were rivals for the Second Master's job, which was becoming vacant at the end of the year. The incurable vanity of each prompted them to believe that, if 'Smith' behaved badly in their presence, it would somehow reflect badly on them.

There was not much that they could do. The conversation had turned to Tennyson. Norman had never noticed these literary interests of Lubbock's before. While Quirk wolfed his second Cassata – a delicacy which, for some reason, the cook thought to be a favourite among the bachelors – Lubbock, still toying with chips from which he refused to be parted, began to recite, 'Whirl, and follow the sun!'

Musgrove was crimson with embarrassment.

'When he was a little boy,' said Lubbock, quite soberly breaking off from this recitation, 'he used to run round his father's garden, shouting "Far, far away." '

'I think that's where you should be, old boy.'

Musgrove was hopeless in a crisis. Quivering with emotion, he had stood up, and was holding Lubbock by the elbow.

'Shows he knew the music of words. That's all words are, music. FAR, FAR, AWAY!'

This was really bellowed.

Quirk's supercilious expression had bubbled into a snigger. It had a tendency to do this when things became embarrassing. Like a choirboy being unable to control laughter during a sermon. Clearly, he intended to play the game differently from Musgrove. While Musgrove panicked, Quirk would be shown up as the detached observer, hardly to be held responsible for a misbehaviour of his colleagues.

'He also liked saying, "I hear a voice that's singing in the wind," ' said Norman. Musgrove was clearly not going to have any success in getting Lubbock to move. Tennyson had been raised as a topic of conversation. He saw no reason not to continue it.

'Don't just sit there, you bloody idiot; take his other arm!'

'That's right,' said Lubbock. 'Music and words.' He began to burble, in the manner so familiar to Norman. The sounds turned to a vaguely familiar tune, increasing in volume as they did so. In other contexts, the surprising sonority of Lubbock's singing voice might have been either moving or quaint. It had none of his usual whining twang. As it was, the embarrassment was so total that the others joined Quirk in nervous laughter.

The night is dark, and I am far from ho-ome,
Lead Thou me o-on.
Keep Thou my feet . . . '

'Take his *arm*.'

Musgrove had become beetroot with anxiety. Norman had seen him in such rages with the boys, so he knew the form. His spotted bow-tie had begun to twirl itself into an unintentionally jaunty angle, and his eyebrows had begun to shoot up and down.

'Shotover, you fool. Sale will be here in a minute.'

Norman saw no reason why he should enter into Musgrove's slavish desire to keep on the right side of Sale. If anything, the idea of Lubbock disgracing himself – and, presumably, being given the sack almost at once – was an appealing one.

Lubbock had suddenly taken notice of the fact that a 'scene' was going on around him, and he stopped singing. He looked at Musgrove tolerantly and shook his head. Among other things, he was clearly puzzled about how the hymn continued.

'Is he all right?' Lubbock turned to Norman with an air mock concern, and then looked back at Musgrove. 'What are you holding my arm for?'

'Let's find your room for you, shall we old boy?'

'He's not drunk, is he?' This time, the whole table was addressed. Lambourne, a chemist who never spoke, looked as if he was eating his handkerchief. 'Not the tiniest, weeniest bit blotto? He's holding my arm very nicely. Perhaps he wants to marry me. Shall we get married?'

'Shotover, *do* something.' Short of actually manhandling Lubbock, it was hard to see how Norman was expected to put an end to the scene.

Lubbock shook himself free, and started to sing again.

'*Keep Thou my feet, te tum, te tum, te tum, te tum.* Now, what in Christ's name comes after that?'

'I do not ask to see the distant scene,' said Norman, truthfully.

'No, it isn't,' Lubbock replied sharply. 'I cannot see what flowers are at my feet. No. Definitely not.'

'You may be right.'

'Bet you a hundred pounds it's not,' said Lubbock.

'As I said, you may be right.'

'*I do not ask to see*

The distant scene: one step enough for me,' said Quirk, who detested inaccuracy of any kind.

'Exactly,' said Lubbock. 'Bet you a hundred pounds. You said it was "Whirl and follow the sun". Or was it the Pole Star? I don't know. God, I think you've given me a drop too much of this sherry.'

'This is absurd,' said Musgrove, raising his voice, and looking about him desperately. 'In any minute, Sale is going to appear.'

'Who?' asked Lubbock.

'The Headmaster.'

'Good. Excellent. I shall look forward to meeting him. What did you say he was called? Snail, Snail, I salute thee!'

Quirk had already smothered his giggles and was waddling forward obsequiously.

'Good evening, Headmaster,' he said, casting a gloating eye in the direction of the embarrassed Musgrove. 'Can I pour you a cup of coffee?'

The sight of the conceited, stocky little figure of Sale, rubbing his hands, brought an air of sobriety over the assembled company.

'Good evening gentlemen,' he said, showing a good deal of teeth. 'I have just been checking the boot cupboards. Would you believe that forty-nine out of two hundred and eighty-six locks are defective? And that is on the south side of the school alone.'

He stopped smiling, and allowed the information to sink in, while Quirk handed him a cup of coffee.

'I counted them,' he added, somewhat unnecessarily.

'It deserves looking into, Headmaster.'

It was painful to see Musgrove cringing so.

'The boys don't lock them properly,' pursued Sale. 'I have had to reprimand more than one offender for simply slamming his locker shut. But still,' he added, as if pettiness were the last thing he could be accused of, 'I don't want to interrupt the tranquillity of your supper-table with these parochial concerns.'

He cocked his little finger in the air as he brought his coffee-cup to his lips with greedy slurping noises.

'Mr Smith has travelled here from Hendon,' said Quirk maliciously.

'Dr Smith? I'm so sorry, Dr Smith' – this was the manner Sale adopted with parents – 'I didn't see you there behind Mr Musgrove.'

All the teeth were visible again. He came forwards and shook Lubbock's hand vigorously.

'You had a good journey, I trust.'

'I came in a helicopter,' said Lubbock. 'I parked it on the playing-fields.'

'Well, well, well.'

Sale did not know how to take this revelation. Jokes – if this was one – did not come into his view of things. And yet he was too unsure of himself to question the probability of the assertion.

'I'll have it moved by morning,' said Lubbock.

'I shall write a memo to one of the groundsmen,' said Sale. 'We can't have you without somewhere to put it. It's not everyday that we have a colleague with a helicopter.'

Once the matter could be seen in this light, Sale was able to view it as a cause for self-congratulation, and he beamed munificently. Clearly, the thought of writing yet another memo gave pleasure.

'You'll meet your colleagues in the classical department in the morning,' he said, turning to more professional matters. 'As you have probably heard, I take the Sixth Form for Thucydides, but otherwise I shall leave you a fairly free hand.'

Lubbock now looked genuinely worried. He seemed, if not to have sobered up, to have moved into a different, more coherent phase of drunkenness.

'Mr Triggs runs the department. You didn't have the chance to meet him when you came for your interview, but I'm sure he'll tell you all you need to know.'

'But I'm supposed to be teaching history.'

The tone of his remark was difficult enough to catch for those who had heard the rest of Lubbock's fantastic accounts of himself that evening. Musgrove's face had gone quite dark with worry.

'Come on, old man,' he said, as if enough was enough.

Sale, coming to Lubbock fresh, as it were, was altogether thrown by this disclosure. For him – who, of all people, liked to 'get things right' – to have appointed a man to teach the wrong subject was almost unthinkable. But there could be no doubt that it all reflected poorly on him, rather than on Lubbock.

'The French Revolution,' added Lubbock. 'I've all the books I need over there in my bag. My God, where did you put my bag? There it is. I've brought Carlyle and Burke. I thought the boys might like them.'

Norman was astonished to see that this fairly routine play-acting quickly had Sale eating out of Lubbock's hand. He clearly did not want to admit to any vagueness on the matter. His self-regard, his supposed insistence of efficiency in every area of life, depended on it. He stared at Lubbock blankly, as if asking for help. The dreadful chimpanzee grin had faded. His lips quivered.

'There appears to have been some confusion,' said Quirk, twisting the knife.

'There's no confusion at all,' said Lubbock haughtily. 'Mr

Snail made a slip of the tongue, that's all.'

'I've no doubt that it can all be sorted out,' said Sale feebly. 'Perhaps we had better go and have a little talk about it, Dr Smith.'

'Musgrove here was about to show me to my room,' said Lubbock. 'Weren't you, Musgrove?'

'Only if you're ready, old boy.'

Musgrove was a pitiful sight. He spoke very quietly. His bow tie, now practically collapsed, looked boyish and pathetic.

'Perhaps if you cared to join me in my study in about ten minutes, then?' said Sale, coy as an undergraduate inviting a girl to tea. 'I'm sure it can all be sorted out.'

He put down his coffee-cup and fled.

'Come on, old man,' said Musgrove, taking Lubbock's arm, and they too, left the room.

'How peculiar,' said Quirk when they were gone. He fixed Norman with his piggy eyes. 'Quite a character, our new Dr Smith.'

'Yes,' said Norman. 'He certainly seems to be.'

None of the Alfonsine cunning had really brushed off on Norman during his three years in the Institute. Lubbock's behaviour on that first night continued to baffle him for a number of days. When Lubbock and he had the chance to be alone together, it was all explained. Afraid that as a lapsed, alcoholic priest he might make a rather poor impression on Sale, Lubbock had invented a doctorate for himself. The pretence that he believed himself to have been appointed as a history master would have two effects. It would make Sale feel immediately guilty in relation to him. Then, when he said that, in the circumstances, and to help the school out, he would be prepared to teach Latin, it would create an impression of generosity of spirit and breadth of intellect. Besides, no one could complain if he turned out to teach Latin very badly. He could always turn round and say that it was not what he was meant to be doing in the first place.

'You won't let on, Shotty, of course?'

'Of course not.'

Norman had assumed, when Lubbock had appeared through the window, that he would feel acute misery and discomfort until the man went away again. But, although he was still irritated by Lubbock's voice and manner, he was almost pleased to see him again. He had been a trifle lonely ever since being at the school, and a familiar face was welcome. Besides, Lubbock seemed somehow nicer, more relaxed.

'You didn't guess that I was running away, too?'

'At the air terminal? It never crossed my mind.'

'I'd had enough. That ghastly old Cassidy. More than I could stand. Then, when they said I was drinking too much, I thought it was time to throw in the sponge.'

Norman did not want to allude to the drinking. It embarrassed him too acutely.

'How are you enjoying the teaching?' he asked.

'It's okay,' said Lubbock, airily. 'Something to do.'

It was extraordinary that, within his own eccentric terms, Lubbock appeared to fit into the life of the school rather well. The boys behaved for him, and lapped up all his improbable stories. The other masters, to almost the same degree as the Alfonsine priests had shown the same tendency, took Lubbock on his own estimation. They did not question the veracity of his doctorate from the University of Illinois, and they all seemed to be very impressed by his ability to teach Latin at such short notice.

Norman would have expected Johnson, that man of common sense, to see another side of Lubbock, and he was right. But the side that was stressed surprised him.

'You must come and have supper with us again,' said Johnson one evening after school.

'I should love to.'

They were drinking pints in the local pub.

'You can tell me about your friend Doctor Smith.'

'My friend?' Norman started. Lubbock and he had agreed to keep their former acquaintanceship a secret.

'I've seen you having little walks together.'

'Perhaps we have.'

This was awkward. Norman could not tell whether Johnson was on to something.

'I wonder what Smith was up to before he came here,' pursued Johnson.

'Writing his doctoral thesis, perhaps,' said Norman quickly.

'Perhaps. But how old is he? My age? More?'

'He must be fifty.'

'Smith? Infinitely less. He told me a story the other day about the black-out in which he figured as a babe-in-arms.'

'I don't think you can always rely on Smith's stories,' said Norman.

'Evidently not. What was it? Helicopters? Even so, he's not much more than forty. It's that grey hair which deceives you.'

'Perhaps.'

'There's a funny thing about Smith.'

'Many.'

'No, but something in particular.'

'Go on.'

Johnson was fingering a beer-mat gingerly, turning it over and over, as if it contained some vital piece of information which, if carefully enough perused, might throw light on Smith's character.

'I'm not sure I should tell you,' he said at length.

'Having gone so far, you more or less have to.'

'It's to do with Mary.'

'Your wife?'

'Yes.'

'What about her?' Norman liked Mary. Her lasagne had revived his drooping spirits on more than one Sunday evening.

'I think most people would think of us as a fairly happily married couple?'

'One of the happiest.'

Norman felt awkward. He did not know anything about the subject. Nor did he feel that he knew Johnson quite well

105

enough for the sort of disclosure which might be about to be made.

'We are. She's never looked at another man in twelve years, or whatever it is.'

'Or you at another woman?' The old technique of hearing confessions still lingered.

'I wouldn't say *looked*. But I've never had an *affaire*. Never wanted to.'

'Nor would anyone who was married to Mary.'

'Exactly. Well, Mary and I had Smith to supper a week or two ago.'

'I didn't know.'

'Mary likes to do her stuff by new colleagues. Besides, she was interested in all the stories I had told her about Smith.'

'And he came?'

'It was a great success. He ate enough to sink a battleship, which rather surprised me. You had said that he was dyspeptic.'

'It must be the food they give the residents.'

'Mary really surpassed herself. We had avocados, and then some rather nice chicken thing, and apple tart. Just as we were all sitting down to coffee, Smith said, "You wouldn't have such a thing as a piece of cheese?" '

'Was Mary very upset?'

'Not in the least. She might have been if it had been someone else. But on this occasion, she seemed to take it as normal; not even funny.'

Johnson paused. Norman thought that that was the end of the story.

'What an odd thing,' he said.

'I haven't come to the odd thing yet. Mary got up and said she was going into the kitchen for the cheese. When she had gone, Smith was very apologetic, said what an admirable meal it had been, but that for some reason, he still felt hungry. Said he would go and have his cheese in the kitchen, and followed her off. I saw nothing odd in it, really.'

'But there was?'

'They were gone such a hell of a long time. I quite

genuinely wondered whether they thought I was being off-hand, sitting on my own over the coffee instead of helping with the washing-up. So I went and joined them.'

He began to consult the beer-mat again for inspiration.

'Was something awful going on?'

'It looked fairly awful. Mary and Smith were having a good old grope in front of the sink.'

'Kissing each other?'

'That's what I mean. The real thing. Not just a little peck. They both looked up when I came in. Mary went pretty red and got on with the washing-up. Smith just laughed benignly, and said how nice it was to come to a house where they kept a good camembert. He seemed quite untroubled by the incident. Stayed about two hours after that, talking about everything under the sun – Shakespeare, politics, America – his family went over in the Mayflower, you know; real Pilgrim Fathers.'

'I hadn't heard.'

'Oh, yes. He's got the documents to prove it, apparently.'

'What did Mary say afterwards?'

'As I say, it's not the sort of thing she normally does. Or, at least, I don't think it is. She was covered with confusion when we were alone again; said that it had never happened before; that she didn't know what came over her.'

'So, that's the odd thing about Smith?'

'As you say, one of them. But he's evidently got what it takes when it comes to the ladies.'

It was slightly embarrassing when silence fell. Norman went to buy two more pints. Johnson was right. He should not have told him all this. When he came back with the pints, Norman asked.

'Is she in love with Smith?'

'Good heavens, no. She found the whole thing funny afterwards. Said she simply didn't know how it happened.'

'Were you all tight?'

'We'd had a bottle or two of my home-made plonk. Smith can put it back, you know. But, no, we weren't noticeably tight. Mary was quite lucid about that. That was what made

107

me so sure it had never happened before with anyone else –
since we were married, that is. She said that, in that instant,
she found him overwhelmingly physically attractive. Just
couldn't resist.'

'And you believe her?'

'Yes.'

'Has he been chasing her since?'

'Look, it's not like that.'

Norman could not imagine why an intelligent woman like
Mary Johnson should have been taken in by Lubbock, still
less found him attractive. Still, what made people attractive
to the opposite sex had to be taken on trust, and could not be
disputed. The quality was something he had noted in Lubbock before – when embracing the dancing nuns at Mass, for
example; to a lesser extent, that night at the Gobi Club.

He was silent as he contemplated these things.

'I expect old Smith has a mistress in town somewhere or
another,' said Johnson. 'I wonder who she is.'

Father Cassidy, in a white cap, flannel check shirt, and white
trousers, drove off into a bunker.

'Let's pause,' he said.

Quirk was out of breath. He did not like meeting at the
golf-course. But Cassidy had said that their former rendez-
vous in Harrow, when they pretended to take lessons in
Highland dancing, was becoming risky.

'It can't be a coincidence,' said Cassidy crossly.

'All I said was that it appears to be.'

'And Shotover is still teaching the Arab twins?'

'He keeps trying to get out of it.'

'A crafty move. With Sale, he can be fairly sure that he will
have sole control of them before long.'

'It appears to be so.'

A distant train hooted. Quirk strained his eyes to see what
sort it was, but it was lost behind some trees.

'We are not paying you good money for nothing,' said
Father Cassidy crossly. 'I want some more details. And, if my
suspicions are correct, we shall need them fast.'

Wearily, Quirk waddled his way up the slope towards the sixteenth hole. He wished that he had never consented to work for Cassidy. It would never have happened if the news-agent had not sent that extraordinary magazine one week instead of *Siding Notes*. He had been a fool to answer one of their beguiling advertisements. RUBBER-DUB-DUB, it had said, with a P.O. Box mumber. When he answered it, he had been bidden to a discreet address in Hammersmith; but, instead of the lessons with a very strict person that he had been so much looking forward to, Cassidy had been waiting for him. And so the blackmail had begun.

'Fore!' shouted the priest as the ball whizzed past Quirk's head.

6

THE NIGHT IS DARK

Johnson's story had bothered Norman. It resurrected the whole business of women. While having no wish to get himself tangled up, he had come to want some relief from the exclusively masculine surroundings of the school. And the thought that Lubbock was enjoying some success in that direction was less improbable than it had sounded at first. Norman noticed that he very rarely came in to supper in the evenings. Johnson was probably right. He must have some mistress in tow. He racked his brains for days to try to imagine what she was like, and who she was.

Coming down Shaftesbury Avenue in a heavy rainstorm at about half past ten one night, he thought that he had found the answer.

It was March, and Norman had been making one of his solitary jaunts to the theatre. These had become routine. Since becoming an English master, and producing plays himself, he had developed rather a strong taste for the drama. For the first couple of times, he had asked Musgrove along, but his unwavering desire to strike an attitude, always the same one, proved tiresome.

'Rather too left-wing for my tastes, old boy,' was an invariable comment in the interval. And Norman would find him in the bar, self-consciously making a pint of bitter 'last', when the show was over. A rather good production of *King Lear* at the Aldwych had been the breaking-point as far as Norman was concerned. 'Wild horses would not have dragged me back in there, old boy. "Expose thyself to feel what wretches feel"? Dangerous Fabian nonsense.'

After this, Norman had gone on his own. He had just seen the latest Tom Stoppard. He wasn't sure that he had understood any of the jokes, but he had laughed a good deal, and he felt happy as he picked his way through the crowds who streamed out on to the pavements, putting up umbrellas, hailing taxis, or trundling into the pubs.

Norman looked at his watch. The rain was heavy, and would probably have subsided in twenty minutes. There was plenty of time for a quick pint before catching a train to Baker Street. He squeezed his way into the first pub that presented itself.

It had reached the stage of the evening when people were clamouring around the bar like sick pilgrims attempting, by the persistence of their incantations, to receive a cure before their neighbours.

'So that's one vodka and lime, two gins, and three and a half pints of DD . . . No . . . Wait a minute. Two vodkas – was yours with lime, Pete . . . ?'

Trying to catch the barmaid's eye against competition of this sort looked as if it was going to be impossible. Norman edged round to another part of the bar, faintly less crowded, and queued up behind an Australian who was buying eight lagers.

Something of a scuffle seemed to be in progress at the street door on this side of the pub, and people were turning to watch. This probably explained the comparative thinness of the crowd actually buying drinks.

'Christ, don't make another of your scenes,' a girl was saying desperately.

And a stocky man in shirt-sleeves, evidently employed by the management, said, 'Out, my friend.'

The friend so addressed did not seem anxious to comply with either of these pieces of advice.

'I want another fucking drink,' was what he appeared to say.

Norman looked at his watch. Several people had pushed in front of him, so that his chances of getting a pint before time was called began to diminish. He did not particularly want to stay and watch the drunkard being thrown out into the street, so he began to push past the crowd which had collected round him near the door.

'Out,' the bouncer was repeating.

At this point, the huddled figure, who had decided to sit on the floor, began to chant out in those infinitely melancholy tones,

The night is dark, and I am far from ho — ome,
Lead Thou me o _ on.'

There would have been everything to be said, from Norman's point of view, for behaving as if he had not been a witness to all this. Apart from the fact that he would almost certainly miss his train if he fell in with Lubbock in his present state, it would have been kinder to censor the episode. But none of these things occurred to Norman at the time. He stooped down and took Lubbock by the arm.

'Come on, Lubbock,' he said.

'Hallo, there.'

He looked at Norman with a totally beneficent stare, which suggested that he was not at all surprised to see him, but could not quite remember who he was.

111

'Let's get him out of here,' said the girl.

She looked about twenty; anyway, much younger than Lubbock. Her rather exotic silver mackintosh, and her very pale blonde hair, gave her the appearance, at first glance, of having been sprayed with metal paint, like the fairy on a Christmas tree. Her eye-shadow was silver, too, and her lipstick was almost white.

She was tall, and evidently quite strong, as became apparent when she helped Norman drag Lubbock to his feet, still singing 'Lead, Kindly Light'.

It was only as they staggered out into the street that Norman began to wonder what he had let himself in for. Getting Lubbock back to the school in his present condition was not going to be easy.

'Shall we get a taxi?' he said.

Although Shaftesbury Avenue was full of taxis, none of them seemed to be for hire. Norman had never got his drink, but something of Lubbock's inebriation must have communicated itself to him. The flashing of headlights on the wet street, the vivid contrasts of dark and brightness like a painting by Atkinson Grimshaw, produced a strange dizziness.

Norman looked at the girl. Her large, unhappy face stared anxiously up and down the street. Norman's instinct was to be asking some question beginning with the formula, 'What's a nice girl like you . . . ?' For all the affectation of her appearance, perhaps because of it, she *did* look nice. Norman thought, rather arrogantly, that only niceness could have prompted her to be out with Lubbock in the first place. There must have been dozens of other men in London with whom she could spend her time more agreeably.

While he was lost in these reveries, and beginning to wonder whether her large eyelashes, black with mascara, were real, she had managed to hail a taxi by waving her transparent plastic umbrella.

'We'll take him back to my place, if that's okay by you', she said, giving the driver the name of a street that Norman had not heard of.

Norman did not protest. It hardly seemed his business to

do so. He knew that it would mean missing the last train back. But he felt suddenly overwhelmed with curiosity; and, more, a sense that travelling with this girl in the back of a taxi was worth missing any number of trains for.

Lubbock dozed between them, as they hissed along the wet streets past Marble Arch, up the Bayswater Road, and beyond infinitely depressing regions north of Paddington.

'Thank God you came along,' she said, laughing gently. 'I can manage it on my own, but it's not always easy.'

'Does this happen often?'

'You know Lubbock.' She spoke in a high-pitched tone, quite educated, but heavily larded with Cockney.

Norman pondered her assertion. It was not true that he knew Lubbock. The longer he was acquainted with the man, the less certain he felt about the question. He murmured non-committally.

'Do you teach at the school?' she asked.

'Yes, but how . . . ?'

'You look like a schoolmaster.'

Norman could tell from the way that her eyes laughed at him that she thought him ridiculous, stuffy, an old stick. Her guesswork had been impressive, but it was dispiriting nonetheless. He was not used to people commenting on his appearance. He had rather prided himself, in so far as he gave the matter any thought, on *not* looking like a schoolmaster. The sports coat poking up above the white mackintosh collar could have been worn by a member of any profession. And the tie he was wearing was not, actually, a school tie, but that of his old college at the University.

'Have I hurt your feelings?' she asked when he did not reply. This made things worse. It was intrusive, flirtatious, troubling. They made the rest of the journey in silence.

The 'place' which the girl suggested as a suitable dumping-ground for Lubbock turned out to be a bed-sittingroom at the top of a tall dingy house between Maida Vale and Kilburn. Getting him out of the taxi was bad enough. When Norman saw all the stairs they had to climb, he thought the enterprise might as well be abandoned.

'Take his other arm,' she said briskly.

She was much better at this sort of thing than Musgrove had been during Lubbock's first evening at the school. She had evidently had more practice. She had put her arm round Lubbock's neck and supported one elbow. Norman did the same for his other side, so that his arm and the the girl's touched each other as they began their ascent.

'I'm coming quietly,' murmured Lubbock. 'What's all the bloody fuss about?'

'It's okay, it's okay.' She kept saying it, as if to comfort a child during a nightmare.

About half-way up the third flight of stairs, all the lights went out. It was one of those lodging-houses where all the electrical devices are on a timing mechanism, so that only the swiftest of foot could possibly climb more than a few storeys at night without being plunged into darkness. It was now Norman's turn to swear.

'Dark, dark, dark, they all go into the dark,' intoned Lubbock. He became no less heavy as they trudged on up, kicking against each stair to avoid tripping.

'Can you still feel your way?' she asked.

'Just about.'

'There's a switch at the top of this flight. If we press that, it should last up the next two.'

'How many more flights of stairs are there?'

'I thought you said you'd help.'

Norman felt like a bad boy scout who had complained to the Brown Owl about some perfectly trifling inconvenience: a leaking tent perhaps; inadequate latrines.

When they reached the next switch, she managed to press it deftly with her wonderfully fleshy shoulder, without letting go of Lubbock, so they got to her door in the light. They leant Lubbock up against a lintel and Norman mopped his brow. He was sweating profusely and his right arm had gone quite numb.

'Don't say I've lost it,' said the girl, fumbling in her Afghan shoulder-bag.

'No, I shan't.'

This was intolerable. Norman had already missed his last train. They now faced the prospect of spending the night on the landing.

Number Six, paper-handkerchieves, lipstick, a purse, were taken out and shaken, as if they might contain the latch-key.

'Oiks!' she groaned theatrically, and confessed, in a way that implied she thought it funny, that they were locked out.

'We could try breaking down the door.' Norman's response owed more to an experience of the cinema than to practical common sense.

'Cheer up!' she laughed. 'It's not as bad as all that.' She reached out a hand and touched his cheek reassuringly. 'Smile!'

'I don't altogether feel like smiling.'

'Saul has a key,' she said. 'I have to leave one with him. I'm doing this all the time.' Norman thought of his father. 'Stay here with Lubbock,' she said. 'I'll be with you in half a tick.'

Norman was struck by her calling him 'Lubbock', rather than Smith, or some Christian name. It occurred to him that he did not know what Lubbock's Christian name was.

She disappeared down the stairs again. Lubbock was by this stage in poor shape. He needed support, even as he leant against the wall. He had grown very pale. When he opened his eyes, they were evidently not focusing properly.

'Are you the Emperor of Ethiopia?'

'No.'

'Funny. Could have sworn we'd met before.'

'You'll be able to lie down in a moment. She's gone to get the key.'

'Who?'

'The girl you were with.'

'Let's get to the bottom of this. We've met before. You're not the Emperor of Ethiopia. You admit that now?'

'I'm Shotover. Norman Shotover.'

'Course you are. Sorry.' He smiled apologetically, with an air that implied that he knew Norman was wrong, but that he was not going to argue about it.'

Downstairs, Norman could hear the girl's voice.

'Thanks, Saul.'

'Any time, baby.'

A little shriek of merriment followed, and then her block heels could be heard on the stairs.

'Saul's in Dave's room,' she said. 'So he took a bit of finding. Anyway, I've got it.'

She held up the key triumphantly, and unlocked the door.

Lubbock at this point lost balance completely. Norman leant forward to catch him, and did manage to prevent him falling over, but the jerkiness of the action was too much for his system, and, before they knew what was happening, he was being sick.

'At least it's not in my room,' she said, without turning round, and went inside to switch her light on.

'Where's the lavatory?'

'Don't worry. I'll mop it up.'

'He's going to be sick again.'

Amazingly swiftly, she was standing in front of him with a plastic bucket, holding his neck. She made soothing, motherly noises to him as he vomited. Norman stood back, glad to leave him in the hands of an expert. He could have come out of it worse, but mackintosh, shoes and trousers were drenched.

'I'll get a mop,' she said, when it was over. 'Help me put Lubbock to bed.'

The room was slightly larger than Norman had expected, and she had 'made it nice' with Bedouin rugs, poster-reproductions of Pre-Raphaelite paintings (Burne-Jones's *King Cophetua and the Beggar Maid* hung over the divan), and a pretty arrangement of dried flowers on the dressing table. There was a smell of cheap scent. Tights were draped over the backs of chairs. Two or three Indian cotton dresses hung on a coat-hanger on the back of the door. Beads, earrings, bottles of nail-varnish, bracelets, deodorants, postcards of Laurel and Hardy or Winnie the Pooh, and dozens of shoes, mostly red or gold, caught the eye wherever one looked.

They undressed Lubbock, who seemed miserable and

116

apologetic about what had happened, but who was barely conscious, until he was wearing only his shirt and his underpants. Once again, Norman was struck by her proficiency. She folded up his trousers as if she were used to doing it every night of the week. And his socks were carried off at once to the little bathroom on the landing. When he was tucked up under the duvet quilt, he passed out completely.

'There!'

She was still maintaining a sprightly composure, but it was evident that she was tired and upset. Under the silver mackintosh, she was wearing very tight white jeans, and a multi-coloured jumper of horizontal stripes.

'You're in a bit of a mess, too,' she added.

Norman's trousers had by now started to cling to his legs and the vomit was beginning to go cold. Her observation could not be denied.

'I'll be all right,' he said.

'There should be some of Lubbock's clothes around the place,' she said. 'Why not change into those, while I sponge your things down for you?'

'I wouldn't dream of letting you do any such thing.'

'Why not? It's all right,' she added. 'I'm not trying to seduce you.'

'I'm very glad to hear it.'

This, like other things already said that evening, was not strictly true.

She opened a drawer at the bottom of her wardrobe and fished out a pair of corduroy trousers.

'These aren't Lubbock's actually,' she said. 'But they look as if they might be more your size.'

Norman wondered how many men she was used to supplying with clean pairs of trousers in the middle of the night. But he was grateful for the offer, and he took them into the bathroom to change. They were slightly too tight, and slightly too long, but it was nice to be out of the old ones. He sponged them down as best he could, and did the same for his shoes. By the time he came out of the bathroom, she had cleaned up the landing, and had sprayed the air with something that smelt of lemons.

'Want a cup of coffee?' she asked, when Norman returned. 'They really suit you.'

'I don't know about that.'

'Oh, but they do. I'm Liz, by the way.'

Norman told her his name.

'Lubbock's mentioned you. Said you were one of the better ones.'

Norman wondered which 'ones' were being referred to; how much of Lubbock's life she knew about. Because it came from her, he felt absurdly flattered by the information.

'Actually, he rather likes all the masters, even funny little Mister – Snail, is he called?'

'He's settled in very well,' Norman said, while she switched on the electric kettle.

'I do hope he can make a go of it,' she said with a sudden intense seriousness. 'Do you think he can?'

It had long ago ceased to occur to Norman that anyone imagined Lubbock could be, on a conventional level, 'successful', or 'make a go' of anything. He realized that he no longer took Lubbock seriously, and it was at once touching, shaming and embarrassing to find someone who did. Apart from anything else, the existence of such obvious failures as Lubbock was in a cruel way reassuring. However feeble his own efforts to get through life, it was comforting to think that someone was managing even worse.

'He's very popular with the boys,' said Norman. 'And with his colleagues.'

'But is he going to stick at it?'

'You know him better than I do, probably.' He took his coffee and sipped it. Rather surprisingly, it was excellent; Kenya blend, made with a filter.

'Has he drunk as much as this for as long as you've known him?' Norman asked, after a silence.

She held up her hands in a despondent gesture, but accompanied it with a little laugh. Norman began to wonder whether she were not a little tight herself; if not actually 'touched'. Her eyes had a way of dancing about as if every-

118

thing were a joke.

'It's awful for him at home just now,' she added.

'Where's home?'

'Hampstead.'

She did not elaborate the point. Though anxious for more information on the subject, Norman did not see how he could pursue it.

'What do you do?' he asked.

'I work for Alcoholics Anonymous.' Again, the maddening laugh.

'Did you meet Lubbock because of your work?'

'Course not. Why are you so stuffy and stuck-up?' This last question followed hard on the insolent reply and took Norman quite by surprise.

'Am I?'

'Are you queer or something?'

'No.'

It was late. The conversation was getting badly out of hand.

'Why do you say I'm stuffy?'

Clearly feeling that she had gone too far, hurt his feelings, she leant forward and stroked his cheek, then she asked,

'Does Lubbock talk a lot about Mumsy?'

'No.'

'She is so determined that he is going to make a success of this job. She found it for him and everything.'

Norman did not know how to reply to this. He did not know who 'Mumsy' was.

'She worships him,' she added. 'It's impossible not to love Lubbock, isn't it?'

'I suppose it is,' said Norman. He had never thought of things in quite that light before.

Once again, she had leant forward, and was stroking Norman's cheeks. He felt that the gesture demanded some response. He had already become powerfully attracted to her. He liked her very heavy eyelids, and their absurd silver paint, fringed with the large black lashes which dripped mascara. He liked the way that her breasts were so loose and

119

full and expansive underneath the bright stripes of her jumper; and the way they bounced about as she spoke.

'Are you sure you aren't trying to seduce me?' he asked.

'Arriving on time for the first lesson this morning was in some sense disagreeable to you?'

Norman looked up at Quirk's extraordinary self-satisfied features. The school day was over, and he was relaxing in the common-room with a copy of *Punch*.

'Hallo, Quirk, what's that?'

Quirk repeated his aphorism.

'I don't quite get it.'

He was in no mood for a conversation. Sale had been rather angry with him for being late that morning. He had said that in future, it would be impossible to overlook such a lapse. In Dr Smith's case, of course, who was ill, it was perfectly understandable. His doctor had warned him against the dangerous effects of early rising. But, for Mr Shotover, there was really no excuse. Someone else had had to take his roll-call for him before chapel.

'What did the Headmaster say?' Quirk asked, straining after a more direct approach.

'He was pretty cross.'

'An evening of entertainment, I take it? The drama went on longer than anticipated?'

'You could say so.'

Quirk sat down next to him and began to turn the pages of a railway magazine.

'Aren't you supposed to be teaching our oriental prince-lings?' he inquired.

Norman did not like the way that Quirk minded everyone else's business. Nor did he much want to be reminded of the Hassif twins. He was in love, and everything had changed. Sale, Lubbock, Quirk, the Hassifs, all shrank to insignificance in the light of this fact. He thought only of Liz; her teasing, trembling fingers; and that very high-pitched Cockney squeal which she had let out at the moment of climax. It was the nicest sound that he had heard for years.

He was not worried now by any of the consequences. Since they had not exchanged addresses or telephone numbers, he rather assumed that it was a 'one-night stand'. That in itself was depressing. But, on a larger scale, it was unimportant. Something had burst. Life once more crowded in; passion, drama, excitement, beauty. Quirk and his interrogations had nothing to do with it.

'I'm teaching the Hassifs in ten minutes,' he admitted angrily.

'How are they getting on?'

'Pretty badly. They talk to each other all the time in Arabic. Now they've got the idea of learning bits of Shakespeare and thinking that will impress me. But their conversational English gets no better.'

'You know them better than most of us now, I suppose,' said Quirk cryptically.

Norman noticed that the piggy eyes had fixed him with one of their endless stares. He wondered what Quirk was driving at.

'No better than their housemaster,' he said. 'I wish I didn't have to teach them. I've asked Sale and he just gives me all that guff about everyone pulling their weight.'

'Sentiments which are not altogether in accordance with a certain person's?' Quirk asked.

'Which certain person?'

'Yourself?'

He laughed and sat back in his chair to read *Siding Notes*. Norman left him to it. The place was becoming more and more like a madhouse every day. It was the lack of sex, he concluded. The married ones were all right, people like Johnson. He had never noticed it so forcibly before.

By the time he got to his room, the Hassifs were waiting for him on the landing. They bowed ceremoniously and let him pass.

It was bitterly cold. Norman lived in a garret at the top of one of the boarding houses. In spite of socks, wedges of newspapers, insulating tape, and every other ingenious contrivance he could think of, draughts still howled through the dormer windows. He stooped down and lit the gas. It must seem even colder to the Hassifs, he thought.

'Do sit down,' he said, indicating two lumpy armchairs.

'Please, sir, hallo,' said Mahomet Hassif, bowing politely.

'Please sir, sod off,' said Iosif, his brother, in no less respectful tones.

'Who told you to say that?'

'Macracken, sir.'

'Well, it was very wrong of him. Please don't say it again.'

The Hassifs adopted their wounded look. The hands were covered in gooseflesh as the March draught blew through the window at them. There was a silence. Then Mahomet spoke.

'This castle hath a pleasant seat,' he said, in a conversational manner. Then he dug Iosif in the ribs.

'Ah, yes. The air nimbly and sweetly recommends itself unto our gentle senses.'

'Really?'

At least their accent was improving. A weary hour lay ahead.

'It's very good to have learnt so much *Macbeth*,' said Norman. 'But how about some ordinary talk?'

'Sir, we no happy.'

'No?'

'Foul whisperings are abroad. Unnatural deeds do breed unnatural troubles. Infected minds to their deaf pillows will discharge their secrets.'

'What sort of secrets?'

'I have supped full with horrors,' said Mahomet seriously. But he would not elaborate the point.

'Sorry to have let you in for all that business the other evening, Shotty, old thing,' said Lubbock melancholically. They were having a walk at lunch-time the next day, over the playing-fields.

'Don't worry.'

The full implications of Lubbock having 'let him in' for it all had not dawned on him. He had begun to think of his escapade with Liz as an entirely independent adventure, the

122

figure of Lubbock on the scene being something which memory naturally, in the circumstances, played down.

It was also surprising that Lubbock should, even by implication, suggest that he had been behaving badly. Norman thought back to the evening, now aeons ago, in the Gobi Club. No allusion of any kind had been made to it the next day. And there had been other, analogous, if less extreme cases. Clearly, he had managed to keep going by a good measure of personal censorship, not allowing the memory to dwell too closely on the night before.

'Liz is a good girl,' he said distantly.

Norman admitted that, at least in some senses of the term, this was obviously the case.

'I couldn't get home that night,' said Lubbock.

'Of course not.'

'Nor could you, I imagine.'

'Not, in the event.'

If it had crossed Lubbock's mind that Norman had helped him up the stairs, been vomited over, missed a train on his behalf, he had not let himself remember it for long. But vestiges of guilt must have remained, since he said, 'Sorry about it all.'

'There's really no need . . . '

'I was wondering if you'd like lunch this Sunday,' said Lubbock suddenly. 'I expect you get fairly lonely staying here all week-end.'

This condescending tone was not the right one to have adopted. People spoke about drink being destructive. Norman could not help finding Lubbock much more charming when he was completely blotto than when traces of his old, cocky, self-pitying self remained.

'I'm actually quite happy here on Sundays,' he said. 'I have a routine worked out. I go to chapel. Then I take my washing to the Laundromat in Pinner and read the *Sunday Telegraph* . . . '

'My wife so much wants to meet you,' said Lubbock.

It was hard to know whether this was intended as a 'bombshell', or whether it was a carelessly timed observation; that he had not got round to mentioning the fact that he was married before, and just happened to do so now.

'Your wife?'

'Do come, anyway. About half past twelve this Sunday. Here's the address.'

He gave Norman a sheet of printed writing-paper.

'Can't stop,' he said. 'I really feel awful. I think I shall have to go and lie down.'

Norman tried hard not to be interested in the fact that Lubbock was married, but his mind kept returning to it; so that, by the time he was strolling up Flask Walk the next Sunday morning, he was obsessed by the topic. He knew that, if outward appearances were anything to go by, it was inconceivable that he was married to Liz. And yet, so deeply had thoughts about Liz come to colour the pattern of his days, he felt a superstitious certainty that Lubbock had come to possess the girl; that, to the many feelings of irritation that the man had produced in the last few years must be added the torments of sexual jealousy.

Norman could not imagine how they had ever got mixed up. She had laughed at the notion that she met Lubbock through her work for Alcoholics Anonymous. But what could have been more probable? and now the melancholy process of falling in love, again, indirectly, Lubbock's doing, had come to upset his equilibrium. All the symptoms of it were present. Every telephone message, every letter, had been seized upon with eager hope, always groundless, that it might be from her. His doodles during lessons had become variations of the letter L – then E, for he felt that Elizabeth was such a beautiful name, and Liz such a crude truncation of it. His dreams had become dominated by her thick, almost white golden hair, and her enormous eyes. And, surest sign of being in love, the jealous fear that he was going to lose her made almost every thought of her acutely painful. Of all the texts in Scripture that he had come to doubt, none seemed less true than the adage about perfect love casting out fear. On the contrary, it seemed to bring with it all kinds of fears that he had never known existed.

Still, for all his preoccupations with his own worries and state of heart, Norman could not help being interested in Lubbock's marital life. It was so unexpected. When had he been laïcised, and what had Father Cassidy thought? Who, a much more important question, in their right minds, would have wanted to do such a thing? And for what motive? Even neglecting the unlikelihood of his having contracted a match with someone in their right mind, there was still the stupendous difficulty of imagining how day-to-day life with the man was tolerable. Clearly, in one sense, it wasn't; which was perhaps why he lived with the bachelors at the school during the week.

Lubbock's warning that things were 'difficult' at home, confirmed by Liz's sympathetic descriptions of his way of life, did not prepare Norman for anything. Domestic difficulties could be of almost any character of intensity; and, with Lubbock, they undoubtedly were. The drunkeness alone, provoked by whatever degrees of domestic unhappiness, must be causing monumental problems of its own.

Whoever Lubbock had married must have been a woman of substance. Norman was walking into a part of Hampstead inhabited exclusively by monied members of the intelligentsia. He was within a stone's throw of the Heath.

Checking the address once more, Norman climbed the large, gradual steps of a handsome eighteenth-century house and rang the bell.

A head popped out of an upstairs window and shouted, 'Dear Father!'

He took no notice. Then the head said, 'Dear Father Shotover!'

It was like being connected to an electric circuit to hear himself being addressed in this way, and he stood rigid in his tracks. He had not yet fully appreciated how much a renewal of acquaintance with Lubbock might put him in danger of reviving contact with the Catholic past. Rather naïvely, he assumed that since Lubbock, too, had left the Catholic

Institute of Alfonso, his severance with the old world had been as absolute as his own. The greeting was accompanied by a familiar tinny giggle and, looking up, Norman recognized Pixie Moon, the girl he had 'rescued' that night in the Gobi Club.

This was intolerable. There seemed a very strong case for legging it across the Heath for Golders Green; catching a bus; pretending the whole incident had not happened.

'I will come down to let you in,' she said.

'I was just calling . . . really no need . . . just passing by.' Words failed him. Anyway, the head had disappeared again, and she was on her way down.

While he waited, Norman wondered if Lubbock had actually married the girl. If so, how could they afford to live in this house? Proceeds, perhaps, from immoral earnings not devoted to the Charismatic Movement, might have accounted for some of it; but not all, surely. Nevertheless, Lubbock's desire to 'spank' Pixie's bottom came back to Norman. Stranger things, after all, had happened.

When Pixie Moon opened the door, ideas of her having become Mrs Lubbock had to be dismissed, since she was clad in the black gym tunic and fish-net tights which proclaimed continued adherence to Father Sporran's order of Dancing Nuns.

'This is such a precious moment,' she smirked.

'Hallo, Pixie. Is Lubbock in?'

'It is really you.' She gazed at him adoringly. It had never really occurred to him until this moment that the journalistic fantasies about Pixie Moon had borne any relation to the girl's actual feelings. Perhaps they had not at first. Life has a way of imitating art quite as often as the other way around.

'We all do Yoga before we eat,' said Pixie engagingly.

She led the way upstairs. It was a beautiful stone staircase, trailing in a delicate curve up to the landing, and bordered with an exquisite cast-iron bannister. The walls were hung with tapestries representing scenes from the life of Elijah.

In the drawing-room upstairs, where the walls were dark green, and there were an abundance of nice paintings, looking-glasses and objects of furniture, about a dozen people were standing around – or sitting or posing around – in a variety of grotesque postures. Two or three of them were Dancing Nuns. At least one of the figures was of indeterminate sex. But there were some familiar faces. Father Adrian Sporran was standing on his head on the hearth rug talking to his cousin the Dundee of Caik, who appeared, in spite of the comparative stiffness of his pose, to be taking no physical part in the proceedings.

Norman went up to join them.

'The only trouble is that it gives me nose-bleeds,' Father Sporran was saying.

'I don't wonder. Great-aunt Lucy always said that standing on your head was bad for you. She said that it stopped the circulation. I don't know about these things. I've never tried them.'

'Hallo, Mungo.'

'Ah, the Blickling Exhibitioner. How are you?'

Mungo often called Norman by this name. He showed the same lack of consciousness that any time had passed since their last encounter.

'I'm just about all right,' said Norman.

He actually felt as if he was about to faint. He had just caught sight of Liz doing the Lotus position on one of the window seats, her golden hair glowing round the edges in a magnificent haze of spring sunlight. It was impossible to know where hair ended and sunshine began.

'You don't look very well to me.'

'No, I'm all right.'

'You've gone quite white. I expect it's something you ate.'

'I haven't eaten anything yet.'

'Then that will be it. It's time you did. Luncheon will probably not be long.'

'Who are all these people?'

'Friends of the family, I suppose. Some of the young women are nuns. Of course. You know. You're RC. I keep forgetting.'

'Not any more.'

127

Father Sporran scowled at him upside down. It looked as if a great deal of blood was running to the end of his enormous nose.

'I didn't think you could stop being RC once you started.'

'I did.'

'Did you?'

'Where's Lubbock?'

'Who's he?'

It was a difficult enough question at the best of times. Since Norman was under the impression that Lubbock was the host, it was even harder to explain. The immediate question of whom he had married had momentarily been obliterated by the multitude of varied sensations which had overcome him since coming into the house: rapture at its beauty; embarrassment at seeing Pixie Moon once more; astonishment that there were so many people – and among them faces from the past such as The Dundee and Father Sporran; finally, dizzy, hopeless, unmanageable feelings of lust and worship for Liz.

'Is Lubbock that awful man who was sick in the bath last week?' the Dundee was asking.

'Probably.'

Father Sporran came down from his head-stand and smoothed his hair into place.

'Lubbock and Norman here are old friends,' he explained to Mungo. 'You mustn't speak too harshly of old Lubbock. His coming to live here was one of my brain-waves.'

'Not a very good one, I shouldn't have thought.'

There was no chance of pursuing this highly debatable subject since Jonquil Yates was at that moment making her stately entrance into the drawing-room. Everything fell into place. It was her house. And it was she – for what reason who could say – who had elected to become Mrs Lubbock.

She had put on weight, and the impression of rather massive volume was emphasized by her wearing black. It was a loose velvet robe, not unlike a chasuble, with golden buttons at the collar. She was festooned with golden jewellery, a heavy pendant of vaguely Egyptian provenance

falling on to her bosom, two vast golden trinkets the size of
key-rings being suspended from each ear. She had a black
wig to match the chasuble, which increased the air she had of
having just played Cleopatra in a rather expensive Shakes-
pearian production.

'Shotty, *darling!*'

The delicious quality of her kisses, quite forgotten, was
now something which Norman had the chance to appreciate
at some length.

'What a surprise!'

'What's that?'

He could not tell whether she was inquiring the nature of
his surprise; or whether, as a clairvoyante, the whole concept
of the unexpected was so alien to her that she needed to have
it explained.

'Your marriage. Congratulations . . . ' He murmured.

'My marriage? Shotty, what on earth are you talking
about?'

'I'm sorry. I must have made a mistake. Lubbock said he
had got married, and I rather assumed . . . '

She squeezed Norman's hands, and gazed far, far away,
her eyes filling with tears.

'Lubbock has come to live here until he's better,' she said.
'His being married must be one of his little ideas.'

'Oh. I'm so sorry.'

'What is there for you to be sorry about? But, tell me about
yourself. You enjoy teaching, I gather?'

'Lubbock has told you?'

'No actually, I bumped into that nice Father Cassidy again
and he told me all about you. I'm so glad you've kept in
touch. Such a grown-up, sensible thing to have done. Many
people would have wanted to cut themselves off; have nothing more to do with the past. But you are so brave, and so
mature.'

'Father Cassidy knows where I am?'

'Of course. It was when he told me how you were getting
on that I thought the school sounded just the place for Paul.
Then that advertisement in the paper seemed like an answer

to prayer. Of course, Paul can teach Latin after all his Alfonsine training . . . '

Norman stared at her blankly as she spoke. It was only after a moment's recollection that he remembered that Lubbock's initials were P.F., and that he was probably Paul. The last vestiges of feeling that he was his own master were being torn away from him as the conversation continued. How foolish and naive he had been to believe that Cassidy would not be keeping tabs on him. But, why, and how, and in what form?

'It seemed perfect,' she continued. 'I knew that you and Paul were such old friends. And, after he decided to leave the Institute, it seemed sad to think of you out there in Ruislip or wherever it is neglecting all your old chums. Father Cassidy thinks I'm a priest-snatcher,' her eyes twinkled mischievously, 'but nothing could be more manifestly ridiculous.'

'You mean, you actually engineered Lubbock into that job so that he would meet up with me again?'

'Engineered is rather a crude word. What is to be, is to be.' Her eyes stared distantly and became watery. 'Some destinies are forever interwoven, crossed like threads in a tapestry, linked in a mystic bond,' she added.

'So it would seem.'

'Have you met my daughter?' she asked, after a short pause. 'She is largely responsible for introducing us to this new aspect of The Way.'

She indicated the grotesque postures of most of the other guests.

'Father Sporran had tried it before, of course, but he is very pleased with it all. It's an extension of dance for him, isn't it, Father?'

The priest grinned, and squeezed her shoulder as if it were a half-inflated balloon.

'When the body is detached from the spirit, the soul has freer range to move on to a different plane . . . '

Norman was not listening. Her daughter. Liz was her *daughter*. He began to wonder how Catholic theologians ever

130

dreamed up the notion of Free Will. With people like Jonquil Yates and Father Cassidy in the world, it seemed the most implausible account of the human condition imaginable. The web was closing about him, and, with almost oriental detachment, he saw that there was no alternative but to submit to the Fates and embrace what they might bring.

'Hi!' Liz said. She had disentangled her golden toenails from the Lotus position and come over to join them. She too squeezed Jonquil.

'Hallo,' said Norman.

'Isn't it great? Everyone's doing it now.'

'So I can see.'

'Why don't you try?'

'My muscles would be too stiff.'

'We shall have to loosen them up for you.'

She was wearing very tight denims, a stripey cheesecloth blouse and, as far as Norman, after almost manic staring, could be sure of the matter, very little else. Norman thought his eyes might fall out of his head. The denims were so tight that you could see everything; the curve of the stomach; the sharply rounded outlines of her buttocks. In the upper regions, nipples were discernible through the cheesecloth.

'Isn't it great, our having so many friends in common?'

'Astonishing,' he admitted.

'I was so glad when Lubbock said he'd invited you to lunch.'

'Were you really?'

'I don't usually come home for lunch, on Sundays. It can be pretty draggy.'

They had wandered apart from the rest of the company so that such sentiments could be given free expression without causing offence to her mother.

'Does she usually have all these nuns?'

'Mumsy? That or something like it. She and Father Sporran are writing another book together. It's going to be called *Prayers at the Bus-stop*, with ways of going off into a trance even when you're out shopping.'

'They've written quite a lot of books like that already.'

'Oh, dozens. It will be the fourth they've done this year. But they sell very well. Not that Mumsy cares about that, but it helps Adrian to pay for his nuns.'

'I've been thinking about you a lot.'

'Have you really?'

She giggled nervously. Norman could not tell whether she realized how serious he was.

'All the time, in fact.'

'You won't tell Mumsy about the other night, will you?'

'Of course not.'

'I mean, about Lubbock?'

'No, of course not.'

'She doesn't like him having these jaunts up to town. None of us do, of course, but he can't help it, and I usually cover up for him a bit, and hide him at my place until he's sobered out.'

'My lips are sealed.'

'Thanks.'

She leant forward and kissed him.

'When can I see you?'

'What are you two doing, huddling in a corner?' asked Father Sporran, coming up and grabbing them both by the scruff of the neck. 'Come and mix, mix, mix!'

He marched them across the room and plonked them in front of two of his nuns.

There was no more chance for private talk. Conversation at lunch centred round a television film about the life of Christ which Freddie Toogood was going to make that spring. Lubbock did not even appear, and no explanation was offered; perhaps it was not needed. Mrs Yates told Norman that she was going to invite him to luncheon often. In the hall, when he was picking up his mackintosh, Liz managed to whisper to him, 'I'll ring you up.'

7

SPITE OF FEARS

Father Cassidy heard on the news that Sheikh Hassif al Hassif had ordered his Minister for the Interior to be shot. It seemed a wise move. He wondered what Shotover had to do with it. He took down a file marked 'Holy Souls', which contained the most important information about the Institute's oil holdings. The General had been on the telephone that morning from Rome. He was worried by Cassidy's fears in relation to Shotover. It was understandable that he should be. The man was a tough nut to crack.

Every move had been so casual, so apparently nonchalant. There had been the ingenious double-take of appearing to be a Tridentine Mass fanatic. That had put them off the scent for some weeks. Then he had got the job, again with all the appearance of accident, at the school where the Hassif twins were being educated. Someone in the world was bound, sooner or later, to want to kidnap those children. Then they could be held to ransom. If it coincided with their father's fall from power and a *coup d'état*, the price of the Institute's oil shares would be halved.

Father Cassidy meditated. He wished that he had managed to get hold of a more efficient informant than Quirk. The man was too pleased with himself, and not, in the event, all that observant. He had not been able to see any connection between Norman Shotover and world politics until the Provincial had pointed it out. Nor had he seen the significance of Norman's having so many Scottish friends. The Dundee of Caik; now, he was renewing his acquaintance with Adrian Sporran. They would probably pay good money to make North Sea oil look a better buy than the stuff marketed by the

Arabs. The trouble was that time was running out, and he had so much work to do.

Sir Alfred Toogood had got him involved with suing a Lesbian newspaper for a scurrilous poem about the Blessed Virgin. There was still much useful and absorbing work to be done with the sadomasochistic magazines. The Cardinal had still not made up his mind about the Safe Period. And now there was this crazy idea of a television film about the Life of Christ. Father Cassidy had told the baronet that there were already hundreds of films on this topic, none of them with the slightest influence or interest outside a religious context. But he would not be budged. He wanted to produce one of his own, he had said, to counteract the evil influences of a pornographic treatment of the same theme by the Swedish film director, Sven Thorlakssen.

He was seriously worried about Shotover. If Quirk did not watch out, the boys would be kidnapped under their very noses. He almost wondered whether, just to be on the safe side, he ought not to kidnap them himself. That would at least stop other people getting their hands on them. The Sheikh might then reward the Institute for having found the children. The Arab world might, in consequence, become Catholic. The Hagia Sophia might once more be in Christian hands; only now run by the Alfonsines, instead of those ridiculous Orthodox. An Alfonsine Patriarch of Constantinople. The idea was appealing . . .

'Sir, you are a gentleman on whom I built an absolute trust.'
    'Thank you, Hassif.'
    'O, full of scorpions is my mind, sir.'
    'How come?'
    'Mackracken and Davis, sir.'
    'What's Mackracken been up to now?'
    'The multiplying villainies of nature do swarm upon him, sir.'
    'And Davis?'
    'He loves us not. He wants the natural touch.'
    'Have they been bullying you?'

134

'Sir?'

'Have they been unkind?'

'Mackracken and Davis, not good, sir.'

'I hope the days are near at hand that chambers will be safe,' glossed his brother.

'But, we can't have this, can we?'

'No, sir. We go.'

'I shouldn't do that, old boy. Besides, you've got to come and have another lesson with me this afternoon.'

'Sir, very good.'

'Excellent sir.'

'Really, it's nothing.'

'We tell you, sir, something very bad.'

'This afternoon, sir.'

'Stay, you imperfect speakers, tell me more.'

But they were gone.

Norman went off to look in his pigeon-hole to see if there were any letters or telephone calls for him. It was about a week now since Liz had promised to ring him up. He had had no letters except a bank statement and a letter from his father to say that 'the croft idea had fallen through' and he had found a capacious house-boat on the canal at Leamington Spa.

Norman minded much more than he knew what to do with – about Liz not writing, not about the house-boat. He knew that his relationship with her so far had only been of the most casual kind. And he knew, in a way, that falling in love with the daughter of Jonquil Yates was playing with fire. But he could not help himself. Every time he passed the Common Room, he now checked his pigeon-hole for post. He lived in agonized expectation of hearing something.

He had even taken to going up to town in the evenings and hovering near the pub where he had first seen her in Shaftesbury Avenue, but with no luck. He did not think he could find her place in Maida Vale, even if he had the courage to call there unannounced, and he certainly was not up to calling on Jonquil Yates in Hampstead.

He tried to stop himself getting worked up by turning his

mind to the problem of the Hassifs. He did not know what to do about it if they were being bullied. He wished that they knew how to speak English, and that they would drop this ridiculous *Macbeth* habit. It was almost catching. They really were most singularly bad at mixing with the other boys, and their attitude to everything was so lofty and remote that it was hardly surprising if they were teased. He wondered if he ought to mention the matter to their housemaster, and decided on the whole that he should not.

The Common Room was quite empty. It was a day on which school stopped at lunch time, and most of the married masters had gone home. He imagined them in their gardens. It was one of the first fine spring days they had had. There were crocuses all over the place. Perhaps Lubbock would be doing the garden at Jonquil Yates's house.

Norman felt a sneaking sympathy for the man. He had not been into school all week. His ailment was described as influenza, but people were already beginning to put two and two together. It would be unlikely that his schoolmastering job would last long. A pity, Norman condescendingly thought, because in many ways he was quite good at it.

Quirk heaved his enormous belly round the door at this point and interrupted his daydreams.

'Ah, Shotover,' he said, 'Telephonic communication.'

'For me?'

'You are called Norman Shotover?' The sarcastic tone was triumphant.

He knew without being told who it would be.

'Young person not of the male sex, I should conjecture,' Quirk called after him as he rushed to the telephone booth by the boot-lockers in the next room.

'Hi.'

'Hallo.'

'Are you very busy?'

'Not very.'

'I thought you might like to come for a walk. It's such a nice afternoon. It really feels as if spring is coming. I've got something to tell you.'

136

'I can't.'
'I cut teaching the Hassifs.'
'That's different.'
'Is it?'
'Don't let's talk about it.'

She stood up and put her arms round his shoulder. They parted at Finchley Road station, and gazed at each other as they waited for their trains on opposite sides of the line; she bound for West Kilburn, he for the gentler suburbs to the north, and supper with the bachelors.

There was time for a bath when he got back; and he was standing in the middle of his room with nothing on, rubbing his hair with a towel, when Sale burst in.

'Mr Shotover, this is disgraceful.'
'I'm sorry. I'll put something on.'

It was typical of Sale. He crashed into places where he was not wanted and then complained about what he found there. Besides, Norman could not see that there was anything particularly disgraceful about being naked when one had just had a bath.

'You were meant to be teaching the Hassif twins this afternoon.'
'Yes.'

He was struggling with a shirt.

'Well, why didn't you?'
'I had to go out. It was very urgent. I left a message for them, telling them to come back tomorrow.'
'Very likely.'
'But I did.'
'It is the most monstrous dereliction of duty.'
'I'm sorry, sir, but they do take up a lot of my spare time. And you did promise me that by this stage of the term they would be sent to someone who knew about teaching English to foreigners. I shall see them tomorrow, anyway.'
'I very much doubt it.'
'Why not?'

Sale was beside himself with panic and rage. Norman

'Okay.'
'How soon can you come?'
'Where were you thinking of walking?'
'We could fly my kite on the Heath.'
'Where the place, upon the Heath.'
'What?'
'It would be lovely. The only thing is, I'm meant to teach in half an hour.'
'The sun will be gone soon. Do come.'
'It's not important. I'll cancel it.'

He put the receiver down in a flurry of excitement. It was wonderful that she should have actually suggested a meeting. It would be madness to put teaching the Hassif twins before the dictates of passion. Besides, they were unteachable. Even Sale had started to hint that they would have to be sent to an expert in teaching English as a foreign language. He returned to his room and pinned a note to the door telling them to come back at the same time tomorrow. Then he hurried off to the station.

He wondered in the train what it was that she wanted to tell him. He was horribly afraid that her silence, and the suddenness of the telephone call, could only mean one thing. And, as he thought about it longer, the fear developed into a certainty. But, looking on the bright side, it would mean that he would have to marry her, and that could not be bad. He did not have much experience of babies, and he rather thought that he would hate them; but he tried to banish the thought.

On the Heath, the trees were just coming into leaf. It was a perfect day for a walk. Liz looked more beautiful than ever, in a very tight, white fluffy jersey, a denim skirt and sandals. Her hair blew about in the wind, and they laughed a lot as they walked along hand in hand.

'Will you get into trouble for not doing your teaching?' she asked anxiously.
'Of course not. It's only some Arabs that I give extra coaching to.'
'Are you sure?'
'Positive.'

They stood for a while and looked into each other's eyes. Hers were large and grey and full of kind laughter. He could not remember seeing nicer eyes, and said so.

She looked at the ground and smiled.

'What was it you wanted to tell me?' he managed to ask eventually.

'I'm going away.'

'Where?'

'Saul – that's one of the chaps who lives in the same house as me – is going to work on a kibbutz in Israel. Well, it was Dave's idea really. I said I'd go with them. I've been getting rather fed up with my work lately. Somehow, it all seems too much, with Lubbock and everything. Anyway, I thought it would be a nice thing to do for the summer – picking oranges and that.'

It was an awkward speech for her to make. He squeezed her hand.

'I wish you weren't going,' he said.

There was a pause, and then she said, 'Anyway, I wanted to tell you. That's all.'

'Why Israel?'

'Lots of people are going to work on kibbutzes these days. Dave's Jewish, and he's got family out there.'

'How about Saul?' Norman asked jealously.

'He's Jamaican.'

There was no answer to this.

'The funny thing is that I shall probably see Mumsy if I go there, because she is off to Jerusalem at some stage with Freddie Toogood to make this film of theirs.'

'Oh, yes.'

It seemed infinitely sad that she was going away. He could feel himself nearly crying, and he did not know how to stop it.

'Come on!' she said, in her bracing, girl-guide tones.

The kite was up in the air in no time. She handled it pretty competently, knowing when to let out more cord, running this way and that to catch the gusts of wind.

'Here,' she puffed. 'You have a go.'

Norman took hold of it, and ran along for a while. It wa much less easy than it looked. Either that, or the win suddenly dropped. The cord became slack in his hands, an before he could stop it, the kite had crashed down into tl branches of a tree.'

'Sorry.'

She was still laughing riotously as she ran up to help, al she kissed him very fully on the lips before turning h attentions to the kite.

It took a great deal of yanking to free it from the entrails the sycamore. When it came down, she squeezed him, a they collapsed on to the grassy bank beneath the trees.

They must have lain there for ages. It was quiet, a secluded. No one came by. He did not know what to say. wanted to beg her not to go away and leave him. He wantec be able to explain how she had brought him a shred happiness, which was now going to be snatched from h But the words would not come. It was she who eventu spoke.

'Have you ever done it out in the open before?'

This was murmured in his ear.

'No. Have you?'

Again, she merely giggled.

When he occasionally looked up, the whole vast sky, so of round white clouds, seemed to heave and swirl in urg rhythm.

'That was so nice,' she whispered afterwards. And tl after about five minutes, 'Isn't it great to think of K making love here?'

'Did he?'

'Oh, hundreds of times.'

'Darling girl.'

'It was getting dark and cold when they moved on.

'I wish we could spend the rest of the day together,' said.

'Why can't we?'

'I've got my Yoga class.'

'Cut it.'

could not imagine why. Lubbock had actually failed to turn up to take lessons in class on more than one occasion and no one had minded much. The Headmaster had no sense of proportion. He was so angry that he actually seemed to be jumping up and down. Veins stuck out all over the place on his ape-like forehead.

'How many times have I told you that the Hassifs are to be kept under the very closest surveillance? We have had embassy staff . . . Foreign Office men . . . the school has been made to look absolutely ridiculous.'

'What's happened?'

'They've disappeared.'

'The Hassifs?'

'Don't you see, they've been kidnapped!'

'They've probably just gone down to the shops.'

'It's seven o'clock. No one has seen them since half past two, when you were meant to be teaching them. The Head Monitor was expecting them for litter duty at a quarter to four. However eminent they might be in their own country, I have made sure that they are treated absolutely normally here, without fear or favour.'

'Don't you think you are jumping to conclusions?'

'Kindly don't speak to me in that tone of voice.'

'Sorry.'

'You plainly aren't sorry. Really, Mr Shotover, I can't think what has come over you.'

It looked as if Sale was about to burst into tears.

Instead, he gave Norman the sack, and went off to have supper with his wife.

It seemed hard that Norman should be taking the blame for it all. It looked as if a plan of some violence had been executed that afternoon. Quirk had been found, wriggling like an upside-down tortoise, pinioned to the lawn with croquet-hoops. The school office had been raided, and a thousand pounds in cash stolen from the safe. Some of the boys' belongings had been vandalized. Mackracken and Davis, little as Norman liked them, seemed the hardest done by. All their money and private papers and belongings had been stolen, and ink poured into their tuck box. And the Hassifs had gone, presumed kidnapped.

As Norman loaded things into a taxi, he thought how sad it was to be leaving the school. Sale would never write him a decent reference after this. It probably meant the end of his career as a schoolmaster. There had been moments of such pleasure: the fourth-form production of *Julius Caesar*; supper with the Johnsons; even pints of beer with Musgrove appeared in a nostalgically rosy light.

It was all Lubbock's fault; or Jonquil's or Cassidy's, or whatever tutelary genius had been quietly guiding his destiny all along. Now, he had nothing in the world once more, and was cast forth on Life's rough seas.

The house-boat at Leamington Spa did not have a telephone, so there was no way of getting in touch with his father; he gave the taxi-driver Liz's address in West Kilburn.

On the six o'clock news, the BBC's diplomatic correspondent spoke of the dangers of an international incident arising out of the disappearance of the Hassif twins. Oil prices would be likely to fall when the Stock Market opened in the morning. Questions were being asked in the House. A public inquiry was to be set up to investigate whether the school had made adequate security arrangements. The man responsible for the negligence, it was stated, had already been dismissed.

Father Cassidy was too angry even to be bothered to switch off when it came to the weather. Quirk had blundered badly. Shotover, of course, had been much too clever for him. He would like to know what the man was doing to the twins; where they were hiding; what would happen next. But it did not do to show one's hand too clearly. It would perhaps be best to involve himself in some other aspects of the Church's work until the affair had blown over.

8

THE DISTANT SCENE

Father Sporran, who was bound for the Holy Land on pilgrimage with his Dancing Nuns, advised them not to speak to Mr Sven Thorlakssen. Some of them had been so disappointed when it turned out that Sir Alfred Toogood's film was to be a documentary, that they were almost tempted to get parts in its pornographic rival. Pixie Moon, in particular, had much been setting her heart on playing the Magdalen. The past, never to be put down, was troubling her. She had confessed to Father Sporran the evening before that she longed to take her gym tunic off during Mass. She had no singing voice, and could not get her mouth round some of their favourite numbers. She missed the late nights, and the smoke, and the money that the Gobi Club had provided.

For Father Sporran, too, old habits died hard. The sight of Thorlakssen strolling about the deck in sneakers and no shirt reawakened a military self that he tried hard to control. The man needed a shave and a hair-cut. Six months square-bashing would do him no harm. Luckily, his English was so poor that it was hard to make out what he said, but some of his utterances were positively offensive.

It was early morning. The sun had hardly risen. They had left Cyprus behind them long ago, and they would soon be there. Freddie Toogood marked his place in *The Imitation of Christ*, changed back into his ordinary glasses, got up and thought about shaving.

It was a pity that his film crew had coincided with two other ventures of a similar kind. And he regretted not having travelled on an Italian boat. These Israelis were doubtless excellent fellows in their way, but some of the deck games and evening entertainments had been excruciatingly vulgar.

Everyone had warned him against sailing, but Jonquil had said that it was unthinkable to *fly* to the Holy Land.

When he had dressed, in a white linen jacket, a pair of grey flannel trousers, and MCC tie and panama hat, he went up on deck and blinked at the sunlight.

The Dean of Selchester was there, discussing the day's work with his photographic director.

'When we get to Haifa, I want to find some slums,' he was saying. 'A few close-ups of a cripple, perhaps, and then a policeman kicking the begging-bowl out of his hand.'

'What if we can't get a policeman to do it?'

'Get an extra. Dress him up in the uniform.'

'Right.'

The Dean rubbed his hands conceitedly and inhaled the morning air. It was good to be away from his cathedral for a few weeks. After his theological paperbacks had started selling so badly, his literary agent had been slow to think of new ways of making money. One suggestion, absolutely impracticable from the Dean's point of view, had been a complete *volte-face*, an avowal of all the traditional Christian values, an affirmation that the Apostle's Creed was really true. It had almost prompted him to change his agent. And then this film idea cropped up. He was to work in collaboration with Benny Goldstein, the famous director. Everyone was making films of the life of Christ. Indeed, on this very ship, there were several crews jostling with one another for shots of the sunrise.

The Dean was pleased with the idea of getting into films, but he had been distressed that the director had been unable to think of a title with a bit more relevance. Goldstein wanted *The Man from Nazareth*. For once, the New Testament contained the relevant words to suit a modern dialogue situation, and the Dean had replied, 'Can any good thing come out of Nazareth?' There the matter had rested until a much better title had come to him – in his cathedral, of all places, when one of the minor canons was reading the second lesson. The Dean had been sitting back in his stall, worried by the frivolity of taking part in religious service at all, when the

words had come ringing down the chancel into his ears . . .
'Not this man, but Barabbas.' A splendid title. Goldstein still
didn't like it, but he would be won round in the end. Barabbas was, surely, in this day and age, a man really worth
making a film about. A man who, in a very real way, was alive
to the issues which affected ordinary men and women in the
street in their everyday situations at that moment in time. Or,
so it seemed to the Dean. Why else should the mob have been
so anxious to save his life? His mind was buzzing with it all.
There would be shots of the Galilean resistance movement,
using real soldiers from the Palestine Liberation Organiza-
tion. Modern dress would be used, and the film would be a
composite picture. The scenes in the House of Caiaphas, for
example, would be shot outside the Treasury in Whitehall.

'When we get to Nazareth,' the Dean was telling a member
of the camera team, 'we might try to reconstruct a first-
century strike situation. A few picket lines outside the car-
penter's shop there, perhaps.'

Freddie Toogood listened with distaste. The Dean had
been his fag at school. Quite a nice little chap then. He
remembered his confirmation. There had been none of his
blasphemous nonsense about it. He scarcely knew which he
found the more offensive, his old school chum or the Scandinavian pornographer. At least it was difficult to tell what
Sven Thorlakssen was saying. The Dean on the other hand
was all too voluble and, in spite of his unfailing talent for
cliché, his meaning was perfectly clear. Only the evening
before, he had been telling the Captain's table that he had
more admiration for Ché Guevara than for Saint Paul. It did
not seem that the man was a Christian any more.

'Do we know that Barabbas came from the same part of the
country as Our Lord?' Sir Alfred asked acidly as he approached his former fag.

'Ah, Fred. Hi. Well, we're not looking for donnish
accuracy, of course. We want to give an authentic picture of
what the actual issues, very real at the time, actually were in
the light of the economic and political realities of the day.'

'And they had pickets in Our Lord's time, too, I suppose?'

145

Sir Alfred wandered away to have some breakfast. It was distressing the way people turned out. At least he had the comfort of knowing that his own film would be very different. He imagined shots of little families riding through Moorish arches on donkeys; or of the wind blowing through the flowers on the shores of Galilee, while he read his carefully written commentary into a microphone.

Dawn was rising over Mount Carmel as they disembarked; the glimmering dome of the Bahai shrine casting a hint of oriental mystery over the rather charmingly dingy Mediterranean port. Mrs Jonquil Yates looked up to it, and, beyond that, to the gorse-covered slopes where Elijah had heard the still small voice of calm. It was all a bit like Malvern, only nicer, fresher, because of the sea. Her eyes filled with tears as she thought of the countless occasions when the Unseen had been revealed to frail mortality on that hillside.

And mortality *was* so very frail. Poor Pixie. And that disgusting Mr Thorlakssen. How were they to break the news to Father Sporran? She had been in and out of the Swede's cabin ever since they left Naples. Mrs Yates wished the girl had not gone into quite so much detail about it. Really, it was worse than some of the things Father Cassidy and Freddie Toogood had made her read about in some of those magazines. The trouble was, it got into your mind, and you couldn't get it out. And she had hoped for such an unsullied, peaceful pilgrimage.

She knew that it would do Paul Lubbock the world of good. He had not touched a drop for weeks now, and was quite his old breezy self. She wondered whether he should be reinstated in the Catholic Institute of Alfonso, or whether he would be better off as a lodger in her house, helping her with her spiritual books. He had had such a hard life. That terrible upbringing in a Welsh mining village, and his mother a famous opera singer who had eloped with Vaughan Williams – or was it Shostakovitch? It was no wonder that he had taken to drink.

She was looking forward to seeing her daughter again, too.

Working on a kibbutz seemed such an idealistic, splendid thing to do, anyway for a week or two. She wasn't so sure about her having gone with poor Shotty. But, after the most unreasonable behaviour of Mr Snail and the school authorities, what else could the poor man have done? She wished that she could banish the terrible jealousy that welled up inside her when she thought of them together. She knew that they were in love, and love *must* always be a beautiful thing, to be revered and respected. And she knew that it was wrong to interfere. Only, she did so wish . . .

Lubbock, in a clean collar and a dark suit, came up beside her and leant against the rails. It was just as well to have her daydream interrupted.

'This brings it all back,' he said.

She agreed that it did. She did not know what he was talking about, but she did not feel in the mood for another of his stories.

'Won't it be nice to see old Shotty again?' he added.

At the Customs, there was a good deal of chaos. Mr Sven Thorlakssen was interviewed at great length, and Pixie Moon was arrested, found to be possessing heroin. Father Sporran spent hours trying to reason with the authorities, but to no avail. Lubbock lost his passport, and had to go back on board to find it. The Dean made a scene about having his pro-Palestinian pamphlets confiscated and his suitcase searched.

The only people who got by without any difficulty were the two Jewish ladies who had not spoken to anyone during the voyage. They immediately made their way to the Gentlemen's lavatories.

It took Quirk ages to struggle out of his corsets in the very small cubicle. When he emerged, Father Cassidy was already brushing his hair in front of the looking-glass.

'The hired car should be waiting to take us to Jerusalem,' he said irritably. 'We haven't got all day.'

'Do you think anyone recognized us?'

'Of course not. Now, please remember that we are here on pilgrimage. We are staying at the Sisters of the Holy Rosary.

The Reverend Mother is a friend of mine – an Arab. She will know where Shotover is and what he is up to.'

Quirk wished they were travelling to Jerusalem by train. There was said to be interesting rolling-stock at Tulkarm, and the points in the mountain pass before you plunged down towards Jerusalem itself were interestingly analagous to a similar system on the old Great Northen.

At Kibbutz Beth Napom, they were enjoying an excellent breakfast in the orange-orchard. They had been up since half-past five picking grapefruit. Norman's hands were covered with cuts, and his back was aching from the heavy bags of fruit that he had been carrying backwards and for-wards to the truck. At least it was better than bananas. The first time he had tried to pick those, he had fallen flat on his face with the weight. He had imagined that bananas came in manageable bunches of the sort one sees in Sainsbury's. In fact, they were larger than sacks of coal, and just as heavy. They had not let him on to the comparatively easy job of picking avocados. He was too clumsy, and dropped too much. It felt as if he had been humping citrus fruit about for months.

Conditions were fairly spartan. He and Liz shared a small wooden hut, where they slept on two makeshift truckle beds and straw mattresses. It already became very hot towards the end of the day, and in the first fortnight, he had had perm-anent diarrhoea. He was not used to so much hard physical work, and he was perpetually tired. Liz had settled down to it all much more easily; so had her friends, Saul and Dave, who now shared a hut with a French girl called Marcelle.

It was this co-operative spirit that Norman found so hard to get used to. Everyone seemed to think one should share everything. The kibbutzniks, mostly Dutch and English Jews, were friendly, but aggressive people, who seemed to have inexhaustible energy. They were outside his hut at half-past five every morning, in their blue anoraks and little sun-hats of blue or orange; and their rowdy songs were still disturbing him at half-past eleven or midnight. Their wives worked just as hard. All the children lived together in a special annexe. Something about Norman's appearance must have alerted them to the fact that he had been a teacher, since they jeered at him whenever he passed. He was quite afraid of going near them. They marched about in groups of not less than twelve, all blonde-haired and blue-eyed and looking like the Hitler Youth Movement.

Liz had worked in the kindergarten for a while, owing to the perennial difficulty of their needing a nanny. But she had given up after a fortnight after a nasty incident during the toddlers' bayonet drill. Since then, she had helped out in the kitchens, and done some fruit-picking.

Norman looked up at her now, as she made omelettes under the orange trees. She looked entrancingly beautiful. Everyone around the table was talking in Hebrew, and looking at her, in what he thought to be rather a lewd way. He wondered what the joke was. He did not altogether like it.

People had been, on the whole, very welcoming, and one did not feel too much racial prejudice. As the secretary of the kibbutz had said to them when they arrived, many of his best friends were goy. All the same, one felt an outsider. The whole point of the kibbutzim, indeed of Israel itself, was hard to grasp unless it was in the blood. One admired all the energy and effort and unselfishness without being able to see very clearly where it was leading.

A roar of laughter went up. Liz was taking it quite well. Norman wondered whether he ought to get up and punch someone on the nose, but decided it would not help.

'Come on,' she said good-humouredly. 'What's the joke?'

'We were wondering if you were going to be another Bardot,' said the foreman.

Liz wiggled her hips provocatively. She actually seemed to like their jokes. Norman could not stand it.

'Why were you wondering that?' he asked huffily.

'We're going to be extras in a film,' explained the secretary of the kibbutz. 'Anyone can help. There are going to be two films going on at the same time.'

'What about?' Norman asked. 'The Crusades, I suppose.'

149

He began to think that it would be rather nice to help with a film about the Crusades. When he had read history at Cambridge, he had particularly enjoyed the Middle Ages.

The kibbutzniks had begun to talk in Hebrew again. It seemed peculiar that they should choose to communicate in this fake liturgical language. Most of them had been born in Rotterdam or Manchester.

'One of them is this sexy life of Christ,' said Liz, slithering an omelette on to Norman's plate. 'That's what made them laugh so much. The other one is all about Barabbas. I expect Freddie Toogood will be over making one soon, too. Mumsy was coming, but I haven't heard from her for weeks.'

'Come and sit down. You've been toiling over those omelettes for ages.'

'I'll just make myself one, and then I'll come.'

She ran her fingers through his hair. It had become terribly greasy. There was no opportunity for washing it properly since the shower-baths had broken down.

She treated him as if he were a child. It was as if, without Lubbock to mother and pet and care for, she needed a substitute. He rather liked it. He had never had anyone in his life who so manifestly wanted to look after him.

She switched off the Calorgas and came to sit next to him.

'It would be rather fun to be in a film, wouldn't it?' she said.

'I'd rather it was the Crusades. I don't like the idea of this Swedish film.'

'It might not be the Swedish film. Lenny can't make up his mind which we ought to act in. The other one is much more Socialist. It's all about Barabbas. But it's less money.'

'Then, if we saved up enough, we could hitch-hike, and do some sight-seeing.'

'That would be great.'

It astonished him that she had managed to learn enough Hebrew to be able to understand the conversations at the breakfast table.

The conflict between which film the kibbutzniks were to

150

work for had still not been entirely resolved by the time shooting started a day or two later. The Dean of Selchester had appealed to the Socialist principles of the English members of the community, and the Swede had caught the fancy of some of the Dutchmen. Since harvest was more or less over, they all trooped over the fields to watch what was going on.

Kibbutz Beth Napom was on a picturesque eminence overlooking the Sea of Galilee; in every way, the surrounding fields were a perfect location for filming.

There appeared to be about four camera teams and several men shouting through megaphones. Sven Thorlakssen, in leather trousers and with a fur jerkin over his naked torso, bellowed instructions in Swedish, which were interpreted by his American underling. Norman did not like the look of him. His thick blond beard and very muscular, hairy body were somehow obscene. He hoped very much that he was not being involved in this production. It awakened all kinds of pious impulses in him that he did not know existed.

'In this scene,' bellowed the megaphone, 'the Roman legionaries have a homosexual orgy. Then they rape some Galilean women.'

Thorlakssen made some emendation to the instructions.

'What's that?'

He repeated them.

'Mr Thorlakssen says that only uncircumcised men are to play the part of the Roman legionaries. There is to be full frontal nudity, and it's got to be authentic.'

There was a certain amount of jocular protest at this. It seemed, in the circumstances, an unreasonable demand.

Norman had no intention of taking part. He could see Pixie Moon in the distance, holding hands with Mr Thorlakssen. He wondered what she was doing there.

'Come on,' said a perky youth, shoving him forwards towards the small huddle of Gentile extras. 'Get your trousers off, ducky.'

'I think I'm meant to be in the other film.'

'Which other film?'

151

Ridiculously nearby, the Dean of Selchester was sitting in a director's chair and shouting instructions to his extras.

'You are meant to be the resistance movement of your day. You've got a very real, very sincerely held political grievance against the existing authorities as you see them. Now, along comes Barabbas. He's a man who is alive to your problems. Now, where's Barabbas?'

'Barabbas is ill today, sir. It's a stiff neck.'

'Well, why didn't he send a message?'

'He did.'

'Nobody told me.'

'What are we going to do?'

'We could do the Sermon on the Mount sequence.'

'We aren't having a Sermon on the Mount sequence.'

'I thought every Life of Christ had a Sermon on the Mount sequence.'

'How often do I have to tell you that this is a life of Barabbas? *Not this Man, but Barabbas.* That's what I want the film to be called.'

'Mr Goldstein wants a Sermon on the Mount sequence.'

The Dean sighed and mopped his brow. What did Goldstein know about it? Why did he ask him along as a religious adviser if he never took his advice?

Mr Goldstein, who had motored up from his hotel in Tel Aviv that morning, approached, smoking a cigar.

'Is everything all right for the Sermon on the Mount sequence?' he asked. 'Have we got the crowds? Barabbas couldn't make it, today. He's off sick.'

The crowds sat round on the edge of the hillside, and the young man who was to preach the Sermon was being given the finishing touches by the make-up artists.

'Are we ready to shoot?' asked Mr Goldstein.

'I still think you should all remember that you are living in the first-century equivalent of a police state,' said the Dean persistently through the microphone.

'Shoot!' shouted Goldstein.

The young man wandered down from the top of the hill in the full blaze of search-lights.

'How happy are you when you are poor,' he said.

The Dean looked furious.

'Cut!' shouted Mr Goldstein. 'We'll take that again. A1, don't brush the hair out of your eyes as you're talking. You're a rabbi, remember, not a fag.'

'Okay, Mr Goldstein.'

The cameras were put into position again.

'Take two!'

'How happy are you . . . .'

At this point about twenty young men, followed by a roving camera and Mr Thorlakssen in a jeep, drove across the top of the hillside. They were wearing nothing except Roman helmets.

'Look as if you are enjoying it!' shouted Mr Thorlakssen's interpreter.

Norman wasn't enjoying it. He deeply resented having been undressed by the wardrobe department and shoved into this helmet. It was too large for him and he could not see where he was going.

There appeared to be chaos going on around him. He couldn't see the Galilean woman waiting to be raped. Instead, there were about five hundred people of mixed sex sitting around on the hillside listening to some sort of harangue.

Some of the other Roman legionaries had set to work raping them nevertheless.

'That's great!' shouted Thorlakssen's interpreter. 'Those screams are great.'

Norman tripped over someone's foot and found himself lying on top of them.

Then he was punched in the stomach.

'That's what you get for making a bleeding exhibition of yourself,' said the man. 'We don't want your sort here.'

Along the road at the bottom of the hillside, the BBC outside broadcast cameras roved over the picturesque scenery.

'Oh, Sabbath rest on Galilee, O calm of hills above,' quoted Freddie Toogood into the microphone. 'Here, we may be certain, Our Lord must often have come for spiritual refreshment and prayer. Wandering over these magnificent pastoral slopes, the words of the Psalter must often have run through His mind: *I will lift up mine eyes unto the hills.*'

Sir Alfred's eyes lifted up to the hills and saw a minor skirmish taking place among the flowers. Someone had upset a camera. There was a good deal of shrieking. For some reason, there were some people in helmets having an orgy. He and Father Cassidy had never looked into helmets. It was too bad, what people got up to.

'We had better stop,' he said to his photographer, 'and wait for all this turmoil to die down.

A Mr and Mrs Dumble, an Anglican clergyman and his wife, had stopped for morning coffee at the Loaves and Fishes restaurant half a mile down the road. Having saved up twenty years for the experience, they were savouring every moment of it.

'Daddy,' said Mrs Dumble, looking in her string bag for the Ginger Nuts, 'wasn't that a BBC van following us in the bus?'

Her husband dipped the proffered Ginger Nut into his coffee. They always carried them wherever they went. Biscuits in restaurants were so expensive.

'I think it was,' he said.

'Wouldn't it be exciting to be in a film?'

'I expect it's another of these documentaries. They do them so well. I do hope they show that one about the archaeology of the Bible lands again.'

'And to think that we are really seeing all these places.'

'Yes. It is a moving thought.'

Today, they had caught the bus from Nazareth, and were going to Caesarea in the afternoon; and Capernaum if they had time. Tomorrow they were going to Jerusalem.

'Mummy, I think we should say a little prayer,' said Mr Dumble, when he had finished his biscuit.

'And then perhaps we can read some more of *The Inward Journey*,' said Mrs Dumble, pleased by the idea. 'I love

Jonquil Yates's books. They are so, sort of, comforting.'

Being a member of the crowd for the Sermon on the Mount was no more enjoyable than being a lascivious Roman legionary, but it enabled him to sit near Liz.

'How much shall we have made by the end of the week?' he asked.

'About sixty quid if we're lucky.'

'It should see us through. We can go to the bank when we get to Jerusalem.'

'And Mumsy will be there. She can help us out.'

'Have you heard from her?'

'Yes. A postcard this morning.'

'Quiet there! Take twenty-three. And, A1, put a bit of life into it. You are meant to be the Son of God, not some down-town worn-out preacher.'

The Dean looked away. The sun was low in the sky over the water. How little, he reflected, film directors know about theology.

9

KEEP THOU MY FEET

It was a bright, fresh morning. At the shrine of the Holy Sepulchre, the Armenians and the Franciscans had had their usual quarrel about who was to ring the bells. One of the friars had been hit over the head with a broom and taken to hospital with concussion. At the Dome of the Rock, resplendent in the early sunlight, the followers of the Prophet had prayed for the bloody downfall of the Jewish state. In the hideous University buildings overlooking the west of the city, three bombs had been defused and a terrorist seized by the Secret Service. In his bedroom at the convent of the Holy Rosary, Father Cassidy loaded his revolver.

'Truly Jerusalem name we that shore,' sang Mrs Dumble. 'Vision of peace, that brings joy evermore!'

There were not many at Mattins in St George's but, then, as Daddy had so often said, 'when two or three are gathered together . . . '

The pleasing English Gothic of the Anglican cathedral was reassuring after some of the places they had visited. Some of the Greek Orthodox shrines were really too, well, *weird*. It was the only word for them.

And the hostel at St George's was a comfort. They had had boiled eggs and dry toast for breakfast, just as Daddy liked them. And some of the people who were staying there were *most* interesting. That Mr Lubbock, with his interesting memories; such a shame that his father, the Archdeacon, had been eaten by cannibals. And what an added bonus to have met Mrs Jonquil Yates. She was writing another book called *The Pilgrim Soul*, which had sounded most interesting, and which Daddy had said they would certainly order from the Public Library when it came out. And then, those enterprising boys, who spoke such funny, old-fashioned language. Daddy had thought that, although they had British names like Davis and Macracken, there must be a touch of *foreign* in the blood somewhere. The poor children seemed at rather a loose end. The Dumbles were going to do some sight-seeing with them that afternoon.

Realizing that her mind was wandering, Mrs Dumble tried to concentrate on Mattins. Really, it did *ramble* so; all those canticles. Daddy only had it now on the third Sunday of each month.

'Because there is none other that fighteth for us, but only thou, O God,' she intoned, trying not to notice that Mrs Jonquil Yates came in several bars behind the rest of the congregation.

After Mattins, there was coffee in the Archbishop's gar-

156

den. No one seemed to know how the Hassif twins had turned up there, of all places. The head waiter at the hotel, and most of the clergy, knew Arabic, and realized that they were running away. Since it was the policy of the Cathedral staff to shield refugees, the Canon in Residence had decided not to alert the police. It had sounded a most alarming story, even though so incoherent. There had been a fat man with a stick who terrified them by asking difficult questions about the railways. There had been two boys who tortured them and forced them to commit indecencies. And there had been a kind man called Shah Tover who had tried to help them by making them learn spells. Indeed, it was all the Canon in Residence could do to stop them chanting the spells as conversation. One could not have people running about Jerusalem shouting 'Liver of blaspheming Jew.'

'Haven't you any family?' Mr Dumble was asking the Hassifs.

'We hear our bloody cousins are bestowed in England and in Ireland.'

Mrs Dumble was talking to Jonquil Yates.

'I always keep a copy of *The Inward Journey* by my bedside,' she said.

'Yes, yes.'

It embarrassed Jonquil Yates to talk about her books. Her eyes looked away. She was wondering what had happened to Liz. She had left instructions with the verger that the girl should be shown into the Archbishop's garden when they arrived.

'And now you are writing another? It must be wonderful to write books that give help to such a lot of people.'

'It is not simply about earthly pilgrimages,' said Mrs Yates. 'It is really about the state of man as a pilgrim. "One man loved the pilgrim soul in me" . . . '

'Yes,' said Mrs Dumble. 'I see.' It was really all rather above her head. How wonderful it must be to be clever.

'There's my daugher now,' said Mrs Yates, with great relief. 'If you'll excuse me. Paul, dear, they've arrived.'

She interrupted one of Lubbock's narratives. He was

telling the Archbishop about his experiences in shanty-towns.

Norman and Liz hardly looked dressed for coffee on an Archbishop's lawn, as they strolled across in jeans and T-shirts, humping two enormous orange knapsacks.

'Darlings!'

Jonquil embraced them both warmly.

'Hallo, Shotty.'

'Lubbock, what are you doing here?'

'Good old Shotty.' He laughed his irritating laugh. 'How's life on the plantations?'

'Fairly exhausting.'

'Paul, dear, they've been acting in films, isn't it clever of them?' I'm surprised you didn't bump into Freddie. He was up in Galilee last week doing his documentary.'

'I hope you didn't have anything to do with that odious Sven Thorlakssen,' added Jonquil firmly.

'He is odious,' Norman agreed.

'Norman had to play a legionary, Mumsy.'

'Well, that sounds harmless enough.'

Norman was blinking at the scene before him. It was like something in a dream. Having hitch-hiked along dusty roads, and driven through rich, brown mountain passes; having had their pockets picked in a bazaar on the outskirts of Jerusalem, and fought their way through the crowded, narrow streets – no wider than a European pavement – and heard the mingled voices of Jews from all quarters of the earth and of Arabs and Orthodox monks, to have come across an English garden seemed almost magical. It quite brought back the old days when he was on the point of becoming an Anglican clergyman. There was an archbishop, in a purple cassock, bending over to catch something said by a canon's wife. There were ladies in printed cotton dresses and hats, with strings of pearls round their necks. There were plates of Rich Tea biscuits, and beds of aubretia.

Even more peculiar, he seemed to know at least four people in the garden. He could not believe his eyes. He had stayed with Mr and Mrs Dumble in the old days when he was

learning about the Church of England. At first, he thought he
was mistaken. They were not very distinctive in appearance,
but Jonquil confirmed it.

'Yes. I think they are called Dumble, Shotty. How clever
you are. You seem to know everyone.'

'But, Lubbock, what are they doing talking to the Hassif
twins?'

'The who?'

'You know. Those two Arab boys from school.'

Lubbock looked quite blank. He had never had much to
do with the Hassifs, it was true; presumably, one Arab boy
looked much like another.

'Not from Sale's school?'

'Yes.'

'Sorry to interrupt,' said Mr Dumble approaching the
party, 'but I've found out some more about those poor
refugee boys. They've got Irish cousins. I knew I'd heard
that accent somewhere before. Well, if it isn't Mr Shotover.'

'Hallo,' said Norman.

'Just wait till I tell Mummy. She'll be thrilled. A most
peculiar thing has happened. These two Irish boys called
Davis and Macracken have turned up, and no one seems to
know anything about them. The Canon over there thought
they might be Persians. They kept talking about the Shah.
But I don't think Davis is a Persian name, is it? Or Macracken, come to that.'

'Mumsy,' said Liz. 'Norman and I have something to tell
you.'

Norman blushed, and looked pleased. A shadow of anger
and disappointment flickered across Jonquil's face.

'Not now, dear,' she said. 'We really ought to find out
about these poor children.'

There was not long between coffee and luncheon. The
Hassifs seemed overjoyed to the reunited with Norman.
From his point of view, it seemed the last straw. Liz and he
had planned their conversation with Mumsy so carefully.
After two more weeks' holiday, they intended to come back
to England and be married. Norman was going to look for

another teaching job, and, if that failed, Liz was wondering if Mumsy would like a research assistant to help her with her writings . . .

'You know these boys, I gather?'

It was the Canon in Residence who spoke.

'Yes,' said Norman. 'I used to teach them.'

'Whither should I fly? I have done no harm.'

'Be quiet, Hassif. The Canon is trying to help you.'

'Let us seek out some desolate shade, and there, weep our sad bosoms empty,' suggested the other boy, and they wandered off to play chess under the cedars.

'You can't be serious,' said the Canon, when Norman had explained to him who the boys were.

'I am.'

'But why should they come to Israel, of all places? It is incredible. If it became generally known that they were here, there would be a most awkward diplomatic incident. It would look as if the Cathedral had been shielding them.'

Norman hoped that he was not a touchy person, but he noted that there was a note of recrimination in the clergyman's voice.

'It's not my fault that they are here,' he said.

'The Archbishop must be told,' said the Canon. 'But first, we must ask the boys themselves.'

The Yorkshire pudding was almost cold before Norman sat down to eat. He and the Canon and the Archbishop had a most difficult interview with the Hassifs. There had been tears and threats of suicide. Since the Canon knew Arabic, there had been no need to communicate in lines from *Macbeth*, but something of the urgency and melodrama of that play still lingered in the tone of the conversation.

'They say they came to Israel because they do not want to go home,' said the Canon.

'Why not?' said the Archbishop sharply.

'Because their father would be angry with them. He would send them back to the indecencies and the Fat Controller.'

'Why did they come here?'

'Because they knew their father could not follow them

160

here. Their country does not even have diplomatic relations with Israel. There is not so much as a consulate here.'

'But how on earth did they get past the Customs?'

No one seemed to know the answer to this question.

When Norman arrived for luncheon, Jonquil had reached the stage of a second cup of coffee, and the Dumbles had already left the table. He looked at Liz searchingly to see whether she had had the chance to talk to her mother, but the girl shook her head sadly.

Lubbock was smoking a cigarette and sipping his coffee.

'I feel terrible, Shotty,' he said. 'I think I shall have to have just a little glass of brandy to settle my stomach.'

Jonquil looked up angrily.

'I said, just a little glass,' he said.

'Would it be wise?' asked Norman. He chewed as he spoke. The beef was quite unlike anything he had tasted. He wondered whether it was camel.

'Did you sort out what to do with those poor boys?' Jonquil asked. 'I do think it's marvellous the way people instinctively cling to you for help.'

'They are going to stay with the Archbishop until we've heard from the Consulate,' said Norman wearily. 'It's all rather delicate. They aren't going to be allowed out.'

'How sad for the Dumbles. They were going to take them for a walk to the Mount of Olives this afternoon.'

'That would be out of the question,' said Norman.

'Yes,' said Liz, pulling aside the lace curtains and looking out of the Gothic casement of the dining-room, 'there they go now.'

'That's impossible.'

'But that's Mr Dumble, isn't it?'

A taxi had drawn up at the main gateway, and Mr and Mrs Dumble were climbing in with the Hassifs.

'They must be mad,' said Norman, and ran out of the room.

'Mumsy,' said Liz. 'Can I have a little word with you?'

'Not just now, dear. I'm tired. I really think I should go and have a lie down. Amuse yourself with Paul.'

161

Liz went to cry in her bedroom, and Lubbock slipped out to buy a bottle of brandy. The Israeli kind tasted nothing like Cognac, but it was very cheap.

The nuns of the Holy Rosary had dark blue habits with black veils. They wore rosaries round their wimples like necklaces. Quirk was not happy about the outfit. Although he had no religious belief, it awakened vestiges of Protestant prejudice in him to be handling these magic beads. Besides, it was effeminate.

'Your wimple is crooked,' said Father Cassidy.

'I encountered complications with collar-studs.'

'Let me put it straight for you. These nuns are very particular. If we go out looking dishevelled, we would be spotted at once.'

'Perhaps if we had chosen a more masculine disguise?'

'And look at you! You've got your scapular on back to front.'

Quirk looked a sight in his underclothes. Father Cassidy made him undress and put the habit on properly. It was a pity that he had to bring the man along, but there was no other way of identifying the twins. He had learnt, from experience, the unrealiability of photographs.

'The verger at the Cathedral rang up just now,' said Cassidy. 'They've left for the Mount of Olives.'

'With our friend?' This was Quirk's habitual way of referring to Norman Shotover.

'With the Anglican parson and his wife. It looks as if they've slipped through the net.'

'Then, there might be some possiblity of apprehending them?'

Quirk thought with pride of the honour which would be heaped on him when he returned to the school with the Hassifs. He would be almost certain of being made Second Master. And when he was, he would thrash the boys within an inch of their lives for causing so much trouble.

The Dumbles' funds were running out much faster than they

had anticipated, but they bought lollipops for the boys before crossing the Brook Cedron. It was a brilliantly sunny afternoon, almost hot. The ancient olive trees threw contorted, sinister shadows on to the hillside. As they climbed towards the Church of the Ascension, they looked back and saw the whole city, enclosed in its ancient walls, and looking, in the afternoon light, as if it were made out of cardboard. The two boys chattered to each other in Arabic.

They spent about an hour of happy, and devotional, sightseeing. They saw the Russian Orthodox Church, the Carmelite Church of the Ascension, the Grotto of the Credo and the Garden of Gethsemane. It was almost too much to take in. Mrs Dumble knew that the Garden of Gethsemane would be one of the high points of her pilgrimage, but when she got there, she found herself feeling tired, and the only thing she was able to think of was going to the lavatory. They had left the Cathedral in such a hurry. They found one at the Tombs of the Prophets, a little further round the hill, and Mr Dumble waited outside for her with the boys.

'Are you two lads enjoying yourself?' he asked. He found that the manner he usually adopted with the Youth Club which met in his parish on Tuesdays did not work with the Hassifs. They seemed lofty and distant, and it was as if they hardly understood a word he said.

They merely nodded and smiled at his question.

The Dumbles' children were all grown up now. Mr Dumble regretted it. He always found himself talking to other people's children when he went on holiday.

'We are going to see the Church where Our Lord wept over the City,' explained Mr Dumble.

'Those lavatories are a disgrace,' said his wife, rejoining them, but she looked glad to have been.

'*The Church of Dominus Flevit*,' Mr Dumble read in his guide book. 'The site of Christ's weeping over Jerusalem was unmarked until the time of the Crusaders who built a church there, but after their withdrawal it fell into ruins. In 1518, there was a Mosque there, presumably built by the Turks. . . '

163

'History's wonderful, isn't it, Daddy?'

'It certainly is.'

'By the pricking of the thumbs,
Something wicked this way comes.'

'I beg your pardon, dear?'

It was so hard to know what these boys were trying to say, and one did so want to be kind to them.

'Tyrant, show thy face!' said the other Hassif.

'Really, dear, I don't think that's very polite. They are only two nuns who have come to visit these places, just the same as us.'

'It would be more sensible not to make any fuss,' said Father Cassidy, advancing on them.

'Good afternoon, sister.'

Mr Dumble did not like Roman Catholics very much, but these days one had to be charitable. And the nuns probably did very good work.

The Hassifs were running away down the hillside.

'Come back!' Mrs Dumble called.

The nuns seemed to be in pursuit. One of them really looked too fat to move, and nearly tripped over her habit. Mr Dumble thought that they probably did not always take enough exercise in these religious communities.

'Daddy, we can't let the boys run away. They might get lost.'

'Was it something we said?'

'Perhaps they wanted to go, too. There *was* a Gentleman's at the Tombs of the Prophets.'

They set off at a brisk pace after the two nuns. They were tearing through the olive groves on Gethsemane at a terrific rate, and the boys were far ahead. It was as much as Mrs Dumble could do to keep up.

'Daddy,' she shouted. 'Remember your dicky heart!'

They were being left a long way behind. The fatter of the two nuns had tumbled over into the Brook Cedron, but the other one was running fast. They couldn't see very clearly now, but it looked as if someone else was running after the boys too. Mr Dumble wished he had brought his long-distance glasses out with him. It looked like that nice young Mr Shotover.

Norman ran breathlessly thought St Stephen's Gate, back into the City. Once inside the walls, the chase was going to be much more difficult. The streets were so narrow, and the crowds so intense. Two Arab boys might easily be lost among them; so might a nun. Norman wondered who she was. He felt fairly certain that she was something to do with Cassidy. He suspected members of religious orders on principle.

All the streets looked the same: the little shops selling Arab costume, copper-ware, fake Roman pottery, leather goods and Bedouin rugs. It was all like one of those emporiums in the King's Road, Chelsea, only half the size and ten times more crowded. Through the middle of it all, men drove their donkeys, laden with sacks of corn and the carcasses of goats. The smell was overwhelming. He caught sight of the nun rounding a corner, and ran on.

She was walking fairly briskly and, because of all the obstacles in the way, it was difficult to catch up, but he did so eventually. There was no sign of the boys, but she presumably still had her eye on them. This impression was confirmed when, turning up a dark alley-way, she rang the bell of a door marked ORPHELINAT DU SAINT ENFANT.

She had gone inside by the time he reached the door, but he rang the bell vigorously. They were a long time answering it.

A sweet-faced nun with dimples admitted him.

'Monsieur?'

'I'm looking for a nun and two boys.'

'Comment? J'ai peur que je ne parle pas beaucoup d'anglais, monsieur.'

'Je cherche une sœur et deux garçons.'

'Votre sœur, monsieur?'

'Non. Une sœur réligieuse.'

The nun sighed. She wondered whether he was a fanatic. They had so many men coming into the orphanage to steal the children or interfere with the nuns.

'Un moment, monsieur. Je vais apprendre la Révérende

Mère que vous êtes ici. Veuillez-vous attendre dans le parloir?'

She showed him into an austere little room which had hard chairs, whitewashed walls and a picture of the Little Flower over the chimney-piece. In a moment, the Reverend Mother was upon him. She was a formidable woman who prided herself on the excellence of her English.

'What can we do for you, monsieur?' she asked coldly.

'I saw one of your sisters in the street. I have been running after her all the way from the Mount of Olives.'

'Indeed, monsieur?'

'Yes. I believe she was chasing after two little boys. I would like, if you would be so kind, to take them into custody.'

Since the general atmosphere was so icy and courteous, he saw no reason to lose his tember. But it was as well to make them realize that they could not get away with kidnapping children in broad daylight.

'You would like the children as well?' she asked sceptically.

'Yes please. They are called Iosif and Mahomet Hassif.'

'Are you their father, monsieur?'

'Of course not. I used to teach them at one time.'

'At a school, monsieur?'

'Yes, at an English boarding school. Peacham House. It is quite well known.'

The Reverend Mother drew herself up and folded her arms. She had heard of these English boarding schools and the type of men who chose to teach in them.

'And you were chasing one of my sisters, monsieur?'

'Yes.'

'Do you frequently chase nuns, monsieur?'

'Of course not.'

'We have a religious calling, monsieur. It is only by special dispensation that members of our order are allowed to speak to men at all. It would be quite out of the question to let you speak to any of my sisters.'

'But I insist – '

'One moment, monsieur. I shall be back in one moment.'

She hurried from the room. He was obviously a fanatic.

Sister Nathalie's suspicions had been quite correct. He not only chased little boys and nuns; he openly boasted about it. Oh, the English. They were beneath contempt. She locked the parlour door and went to telephone the police.

It had not taken long to shake off Shotover. Nor to catch up with the boys. Cassidy found them hiding in a shop that sold goatskins. Their teeth were chattering with fright, but that did not stop one of them biting his arm in the taxi.

'It's for your own good,' he kept repeating. 'We can't have boys like you running loose in the streets, now, can we?'

He had taken them at once to the British Consulate. The Consul was an old friend of the Catholic Institute of Alfonso. Father Cassidy had received him into the church just after the war. He was a quiet, sentimental man. He fully saw the force of all Cassidy's arguments. No one would want the presence of the Hassif twins in Jerusalem exposed. It would be intensely embarrassing for the Israeli government, and they would doubtless welcome any opportunity to hush it up. Nor was it immediately possible to see what capital the Arab world would make out of the incident, even if it were to become widely heard about. The sooner the children were out of the country the better. Once Mr Quirk was found, they would all be driven to the airport, and the Minister for the Interior had given instructions that their party should be granted diplomatic immunity.

It was still difficult to see why they had chosen to come here in the first place, or how they had got past the Customs. Father Cassidy did not trouble the Consul with his own explanation of these events. It had all become crystal clear to him when he had seen the boys chatting to the Anglican parson and his wife. Shotover's arrival in the Catholic Institute of Alfonso had been a put-up job by the Church of England. It amazed the Provincial that he had not thought of it before. It was the obvious explanation. He did not quite see how the details of it all worked out, but obviously they would take any opportunity of doing down their Roman Catholic rivals. That was why Shotover had seemed so consistently hostile to the Holy Father. And that was why he was so anxious to destroy the price of the Institute's oil shares. He must have known how difficult it was for the Church to survive. They had no old endowments, like the Anglicans. It was as much as they could do to get by on such sources of income as Bingo and the Gobi Club.

Thought of the Gobi Club reminded Father Cassidy of Pixie Moon. He had hoped that by planting heroin in her suitcase it would be the end of her. It was most necessary that she should not appear in Sven Thorlakssen's film. It would not do to get the Church a bad name.

'And then,' said Mrs Dumble, 'they just ran off. I couldn't keep up with them, and Daddy really shouldn't have run as much as he did. He has a dicky heart, you know.'

'So do I,' said Lubbock. He was feeling much better after half a bottle of brandy.

'But what happened to Norman?' asked Liz anxiously.

'Well, as I say,' said Mr Dumble, 'I couldn't be sure that it was Norman. I didn't have my long-distance glasses.'

'He's been gone ever since lunch-time,' said the girl. She was on the point of tears.

'And here we are lingering over tea,' said Mrs Dumble obviously. 'I must go and powder my nose before Evensong.'

Lubbock hiccoughed.

'But, hey, this is serious,' said Liz.

No one seemed to understand. Norman had been going to help. Someone had kidnapped the kids, and no one seemed to be taking any notice. The Dumbles had left the little lounge where they were all sitting, and she found herself alone with Lubbock. She was worried. Something told her that everything was going badly wrong. She wished that Mumsy would come out of her bedroom and be more sympathetic. She could not understand her attitude. She must have guessed what Norman and she wanted to tell her, but she was just not allowing them to say it.

'I might go and sing a few hymns,' said Lubbock.

'Oh, Christ, you've been drinking again,' she said angrily,

and burst into paroxysms of tears and panic.

'I wish to see the British Consul. This is all quite outrageous.'

'We are flying you to Cyprus. You can make your own way home from there.'

'But I don't want to go home. I have got friends here. They are staying at St George's Cathedral.'

'If you wish to give me your friend's name and address, I can have a message sent to him.'

'It's a her.'

The policeman raised his eye-brows and smiled.

'A nun?' he asked.

'No. It's my fiancée.'

'Ah!' There seemed almost a note of sadness in his voice.

Norman wrote Liz's name on a piece of paper for the policeman.

'Your plane departs in half an hour,' he was told. 'I am going to stamp your passport for you now.'

He produced a large rubber stamp from a desk-drawer, carefully inked it, and then brought it down heavily on the little blue book. Then he handed it back to Norman.

Across the details of his height, age, colouring and profession was the single word PAEDERAST.

'I insist that you rub it out,' he spluttered.

'I am sorry, sir. If you behave like that in our country, you must expect what you deserve.'

He picked up the piece of paper, looked at Liz's name sadly, and left the room.

In another part of the airport, Quirk, Cassidy and the Hassifs boarded a plane for Italy.

'Is Shotty still not back?' asked Jonquil Yates, when she appeared for supper. She had finished another chapter of *The Pilgrim Soul* and was feeling hungry. She tucked into her cold camel and salad with unfeeling gusto.

Liz, pale and red-eyed, was not eating anything.

'I think we ought to call the police.'

'Where's Paul?'

'He's in his bedroom,' said Liz truthfully. 'He wasn't feeling very well.'

'What a shame. He has been eating so well lately, too. There was quite a touch of colour in his cheeks this morning.'

'Mumsy, there's something I want to talk to you about. I know you don't want to talk about it, but we must.'

'After supper, dear,' she said.

But after supper, she suggested that they went upstairs to her bedroom to listen to the news on the World Service. After Lilla-Burlero Bullen-a-la-la came the comforting BBC announcer's voice.

'The Hassif twins, children of the Arab oil magnate Sheikh Hassif al Hassif, have been found. They have been rescued by a master from their school in London and by Father Aloysius Cassidy, Provincial of the Catholic Institute of Alfonso. Here is our Rome Correspondent.'

'That must be Norman!' The girl looked puzzled, but proud.

'Ssh, dear!'

'The Hassif mystery is over,' said the Rome correspondent. 'Embassy staff speaking on behalf of Sheikh Hassif al Hassif say that any talk of kidnapping must be ruled out completely. The boys appear to have taken a holiday in Italy without telling the school authorities. A spokesman said an hour ago that they would never have been found if it had not been for the tireless ingenuity of Father Aloysius Cassidy, head of the Alfonsine Order in England and Wales. He, and Mr Arthur Quirk, a master at the school where the boys are being educated, tracked down the twins on the Spanish Steps in Rome late this afternoon. Father Cassidy is reported as saying that the boys were very bewildered, but very glad to see them . . .'

Jonquil Yates turned off the wireless.

'Well', she said. 'Shotty must have been wrong. It can't have been the Hassif twins who were here after all.'

'But he *knew* them, He *taught* them.'

'But if they were in Rome this afternoon, dear, how could they have been in Jerusalem at the same time?'

170

Mrs Jonquil Yates had heard of stranger things happening but she was not going to admit as much to her daughter. She did *not* want her to marry dear Shotty. It would be so very unsuitable.

'I thought it might be Norman when they said a master at the boys' school.'

'Again, dear, you seem to be forgetting that the boys were found in Italy. It would be hardly very likely that they would come to Israel in the present circumstances, would it? After all, their father *is* committed to overthrowing the Jewish state.'

There was a knock at the door, and the head waiter appeared.

'Excuse me,' he said, 'but the police are downstairs. They are asking for Miss Elizabeth Yates.'

'Me?'

'I'll go and see what they want, dear. You wait here.'

'But they want to see me. It's something to do with Norman. He's had an accident. He's . . . '

She had already started to cry. Her mother left her sitting on the edge of the bed while she went to deal with the policeman.

When she came back, she was smiling.

'Lizzie, dear, I'm afraid this is going to be rather a shock for you.'

10

ONE STEP ENOUGH

The cuckoo returned to Mayfair before Father Cassidy, but only just. He came back very pleased with the success of his venture. Mr Quirk had been dispatched to the school with the twins, and had sent him a post-card to say that he had been appointed as Second Master. It was of no concern to the Provincial.

While in the Holy City, he had enjoyed more than one audience with the successor of St Peter. The Holy Father had expressed interest in all that he was told, and said that in future, the Holy See would view with caution any ecumenical approaches from the Church of England. He was, he said, bitterly distressed to learn that Anglican paederasts had been willing to go to such lengths to thwart the purposes of the Holy Office. The threat of violence to the Orphanage of the Holy Child was as disturbing as the attempted kidnap of the Arab twins. It had never occurred to him, during a recent encounter with the Archbishop of Canterbury, that these devious Protestants, with their pseudo-sacraments, could sink so low.

Actually, Cassidy was relieved. It could have been much worse. He had orginally supposed Shotover was mixed up with the KGB. He had no difficulty in securing laïcization papers for the man.

When he returned to London and inspected Norman's room with the Bursar, they found yet more evidence of sexual perversion. What could he have been wanting with a woman's fur coat? The cine camera spoke for itself, as did the very manifestly phallic cigars. The skis baffled the Bursar, but Father Cassidy hinted that he knew things which the Scandinavians had been heard to do with them.

While he was about it, the Provincial also made arrangements for Lubbock to be given the boot. The drink problem was not one which the Institute could be expected to bear indefinitely; and his alliance with Jonquil Yates was, Cassidy now saw, highly suspect. She seemed harmless enough, and Father Adrian Sporran, of course, thought highly of her. But it was not safe to trust any member of the Church of England any more.

There was much work to be done. The Prime Minister was speaking of an autumn election, and Father Cassidy did not particularly care for the notion.

Norman had been surprised that Liz should have been so unwilling to listen to reason. Nothing he said would convince her that it had all been a monstrous mistake. There was the word, stamped across his passport; and she appeared to believe it.

'Mumsy said she always knew you were a bit like that.'

'But, I keep telling you, the boys *were* the Hassifs.'

'In that case, how did they come to be in Italy at the moment that you were supposed to be chasing them through the streets of Jerusalem?'

'I don't know.'

'What's the point of lying?'

'I'm not lying.'

She resented his attempts at self-justification. She felt insulted by it. It made a mockery of all their lovemaking, all their plans. Mumsy had told her that he had confessed, long ago, in an Italian restaurant, that he went to bed with boys and wanted to leave the Institute for that reason.

'Let's try and forget the whole thing,' he said.

Liz thought, for the first time, what a smug voice he had. His arrogance was quite repulsive.

'It's really all quite funny if you look at it one way,' he added.

'Ha bloody ha.'

'Don't be like that.'

'Oh, sod off,' she said.

A month or so later, she found herself to be pregnant and hastily married one of the boys from West Kilburn – Dave, or Saul, or Peter, or Phil – Norman forgot which. Jonquil was very understanding about it all, and bought them a house in Cardiganshire, where her husband wanted to live self-sufficiently.

Surprisingly enough, although she had appeared to say such cruel things about Norman to her daughter, Jonquil could not have been nicer to him. He had tried several times to get out of living with her in Hampstead, but his total penury made it rather hard to refuse.

'I know that you and Paul are such friends,' she said. 'I can look after you both, and you can be research assistants to pay for your keep. I really want to start work on a large book this time – a complete survey of the English mystical tradition.'

It was almost as if Jonquil liked the men in her life to have some peccadilloes to which she could turn a forgiving eye; something unwholesome and addictive. She never for a moment suggested that she believed Norman's account of what had happened in Jerusalem. The sparkle in her eye as he repeated the nightmarish narrative was the same as when Lubbock told one of his 'little stories'.

So life continued until the leaves on Hampstead Heath turned a dark and dusty green from the heat of late June. Norman waded through *The Scale of Perfection, The Cloud of Unknowing, The Revelations of Divine Love* and the saccharine effusions of Richard Rolle. Lubbock, with his better Latin, read St Bernard of Clairvaux.

The author of *The Cloud of Unknowing* made most sense to Norman. The notion that all life's evils should be placed beneath a cloud of forgetting was, during those weeks, a helpful one, even though he chose to implement it in a way not intended by the medieval author. Lubbock's companionship made this inevitable. However much Jonquil limited their pocket money and locked up the drinks cabinet, there were always ways of getting hold of the stuff. The haze it produced, if taken first thing in the morning and imbibed continually at hourly intervals through the day, was far from disagreeable. True, it seemed to do no good to his digestion. He found himself talking about this side of life as often as Lubbock had done in the old days. He even began to wonder whether he had an ulcer. If he could have got round to it, he would have seen the specialist. But, somehow, it was difficult to make telephone calls or write letters any more. He kept meaning to, and then he forgot. Then he would have a little drink, and Jonquil would come and talk to him about Lady Julian or Margery Kempe, and that was it. It was bedtime before you knew where you were.

All kinds of worries and fears sank beneath the cloud of forgetting. The juvenile notion that life consisted of a series of choices, for instance, was something that he soon found had been discarded. Things just happened. He did not make them happen. He had even stopped wondering who *did*. Nor did he much care any more about whether he liked people or not. It did not matter. He hardly saw anyone except Lubbock and Jonquil.

He forgot that he had ever disliked Lubbock. It was not a sensible way of looking at things. Just when you thought the drink had run out, Lubbock would pawn another silver ashtray and ensure a few more days of oblivion. He was quite generous with the stuff. It was really rather interesting, comparing notes about their ulcers.

As for Jonquil, although Norman discovered quite early that he was afraid of her, it was impossible not to adore her as well. The stricter the limitations which she imposed on his life, the more he wanted to be petted and minded and forgiven. She always came to see him in his bedroom now before he went to sleep. By this stage of day, it was comforting to lie back on the pillows and let her stroke his forehead, and, while she held his hand, listen to her flow of talk.

'Oh, Shotty, I can smell your breath. Have you been naughty again? Why do you do it, Shotty, dear?'

'I don't know.'

'Promise Mumsy that you won't have anything to drink tomorrow.'

'I promise.'

She would then take him in her arms, and another of those moist, overpowering kisses would be pressed on to his mouth. He would feel the throbbing of her heart through the velvet or the gold lamé. And he would fall asleep.

By the time that she had written a hundred and twenty thousand words on the English mystics, she felt it was time for another interview with her publishers. And this feeling was confirmed when a letter arrived from her editor saying that he was very worried by the whole idea.

175

'Monstrous little man!' she exclaimed at the breakfast table. She had taken to wearing the combination of black and gold more and more, so that in her anger she increasingly resembled Cleopatra. 'Evelyn Underhill has had her day, as he agreed when we last spoke about the scheme. I'm obviously the person to write this book, and it is a book which *must* be written. I shall go up to see him as soon as he gets into the office.'

'Perhaps he thinks it's going to be too long,' ventured Norman.

'Long? Shotty, what are you thinking of? Von Hügel runs into two fat volumes, and I don't see why I shouldn't do the same. Now, will you two boys be good if I leave you on your own at lunch-time? Mrs Fetlock has cooked a pie and will leave it for you on the kitchen table. Be sure and eat it.'

Her eyes glinted mischievously at the thought of all the naughtiness they might get up to; of all the kindness with which she could smother them when they did so; of all the selfless forgiveness she would display.

As soon as she was out of the house, accordingly, Lubbock produced the whisky. Norman had had a bad day previously, and he did not actually feel like drinking much. But after the first two of three glasses, that magnificent warm haze came back to him and the headache stopped. His stomach stopped vibrating, and he felt he must have been mistaken if he believed Lubbock had bad breath.

'I needed that,' said Lubbock, belching rather repulsively. Norman barely noticed. He didn't know what it was, but there was something you couldn't help liking about old Lubbock.

'Lubbock,' he heard himself saying, 'you've been a real pal to me.'

'And you've been a real pal to me, Shotty, old son. And do you know who's been the best pal of all to us both?'

'No?'

'This dear old bottle.'

He brandished it in the air. As he did so, Norman wondered why there was so little in it. It had been nearly full a moment or two ago. And he had never seen a bottle with wings before. It really seemed to be flying.

Also, he could not remember coming out. But, there they were. In the street, by the look of things. Last time he had been aware of anything, they had been sitting in Jonquil's sitting-room.

'Do you know what I feel like?' Lubbock asked, as Hampstead High Street flew bafflingly into the air.

'No, but I know what I feel like.'

'I wonder if it's the same as what I feel like.'

Really, Lubbock was very amusing. It was difficult to stop laughing. It was almost equally difficult to stop falling over. It was these pavements; the way they wouldn't keep still.

'Just a little drink.'

'Just a quick one,' Norman agreed.

'Then we must get back to the mystics.'

Why was this so hilarious? It was the funniest thing Norman had ever heard in his life.

They had drinks in all the pubs on one side of the street. It was after they had decided to cross over and get a drink at the Post Office that everything went blank.

'Would you like a little drink?'

'I don't mind if I do.'

'Ovaltine or Bovril?'

'Bovril. No soda, please. Just a little ice.'

'Don't stay too long. As you can see, he's still not quite himself.'

He opened his eyes. The Dundee of Caik was standing there with a Jamaican woman. Norman wondered what they were doing.

'I brought you a few books,' said the Dundee. 'This is a rather amusing account of the Gothic revival. You've probably read it before. And these memoirs are rather good. One of my great-uncles is mentioned in the penultimate chapter.'

'Thank you very much.'

'Would you like me to hand you your Bovril?'

'What?'

'Your Bovril.'

'No thanks.'

'All that machinery looks very impressive,' said Mungo nervously.

Norman looked up. Someone had hung a plaster leg over his bed on a pulley. It seemed an odd thing to have done. Then he realized he was attached to it.

'How long have I been here?' he asked.

'About a fortnight. Do you mind if I eat one of your grapes?'

'Not at all.'

'You're as well off in here, as far as I can see. It's been raining all week. Some people say that the gardens need it, but I don't have a garden.'

'No.'

Norman wondered if the Dundee had gone mad.

'Should one have a garden? I just can't make up my mind. Lawns need mowing, don't they?'

'Unless you just let them grow.'

'I hadn't thought of that.'

Norman moved his head slightly. Everything was suddenly brought into some kind of perspective by this almost coherent exchange.

'Good God, I'm in hospital.'

'I think that's enough now', said the Jamaican lady appearing again. 'You can come and see him tomorrow.'

'I've left him some books,' said the Dundee. He waved and walked off down the ward. Norman was nearly crying. He wanted him to come back, and explain everything.

The next time he woke up, he felt much better. Jonquil was sitting by his bed, her hands clasped in a gesture which suggested that they were stuck together and she badly wanted to separate them. She had evidently been praying.

'Dear Shotty.'

She stroked his forehead.

'Where's Lubbock?' Norman asked.

Her face looked sad, and she did not say anything.

178

'Dead?'

'Only, that's not a word we use, is it, dear Shotty? They are closer to us there than when we think we see their tangible substance.' She spoke softly, her eyes filling with tears in their usual automatic way.

'Was I nearly dead?'

'Very nearly.'

She produced a handkerchief.

He felt a mixture of awe, relief, and acute disappointment. It would have been so much easier. What was it that he had once made the Fifth Form learn by heart? *To cease upon the midnight with no pain.*

'Was there an accident?'

'You both walked in front of a bus.'

'Where?'

'In the High Street. Paul was killed instantly.'

'Oh.'

She had taken his hand and was fondling it helplessly. It was difficult for either of them to know what to say.

'You know, Shotty, I don't think you ever realized what Paul was to me?'

Then they sat in silence until the end of visiting time.

'You could have been killed.'

'Easily, Dad.'

'You must be barmy.'

It was on a Sunday morning that his father had appeared at the hospital. Norman was struck by the fact that all his visitors, as they had picked their way through the ward, had looked more comically themselves than ever. It was almost as if they were all putting on an elaborate act of self-parody. The Colonel was wearing his brown smoking-jacket and very bright check trousers. He had just bought a pink shirt in the sales which went nicely with his regimental tie.

'The other bloke perished.'

'Yes.'

'You ought to look where you're going.'

'Yes, Dad.'

'I suppose you left the schoolteaching job?'

'Yes.'

'Your Uncle Roderick usually found that a few terms at each school was as long as it could last.'

Norman wondered if his father knew about the word on his passport; whether it was worth trying to explain that he had not been given the sack for the same sort of reasons as his Uncle Roderick . . .

'You'll soon find another job,' said the Colonel. 'One of these agencies. Your Uncle Roderick was always on their books. Taught quite a range of things by the end. They're quite tolerant about . . . ' His voice trailed away.

'How's the house-boat?' Norman asked.

'What house-boat?'

'I thought you bought one.'

'I never moved in. The bloke who built that boat wants shooting. He must have been bonkers. There was no possibility of getting a Bechstein grand into the cabin. The removal men wanted to take it to bits, but I told them that if they did that, they would never be able to put it together again. Of course, since your Uncle Roderick perished, there's no one to play it. But that isn't the point.'

Norman felt too shy to ask where his father was living now. He knew that the old man would not want a convalescent son about the place anyhow. *Where* he was seemed scarcely important. The Colonel had achieved before death some of the qualities which Jonquil attributed to the departed spirits. Place, even, to a certain extent, time, ceased to matter. Their haecceity had been immortalized, and existed independent of the elements or any such sublunary and fleeting illusions as sons or a fixed address in the telephone book.

'Well, good luck with the next job,' said the Colonel. 'And don't go walking under any more buses.'

He sauntered back through the ward, whistling, and with a spring in his step.

By the time the plaster was off, and the horrific implications of the accident had begun to dawn on Norman, it was time to go home. Convalescence in Hampstead was the only option open to him.

Jonquil described herself as having sacked her publisher, and was writing a condensed version of the survey of the mystics which her agent thought could easily find a place on the lists of some more enlightened firm. Norman sat morosely in her study with her for most of the day, occasionally stirring himself to read passages aloud to her. He did not remember a time when he had felt more languid, useless or depressed.

He did not really miss Lubbock, and he had not gone back to drinking. Everything was as sharp and clear as the edge of a dark cloud. He could not remember how he had ever fallen in with Jonquil. There had been the night at the Gobi Club. A luncheon at a restaurant. A few meetings after that. Before he realized it, she was speaking as if they had been friends for life. It was not that he disliked her. As the days passed, and his dependence on her increased, he came to worship her all the more. But it was hard to see where it was leading. And, for all her kindness and goodness, her companionship did nothing to relieve the gloom.

'It's just typical convalescent melancholia,' she said, when he confessed this to her. 'Everyone feels depressed after they have come out of hospital. When I've got this book ready for the press I am going to take you on a cruise.'

'But I need to *do* something.'

'Why can't you just stay here with me, Shotty, dear? Why do you have to be so restless? You know that I need a research assistant, and I can feed you and clothe you and give you a small allowance for anything else you needed. I don't honestly feel that you are strong enough to go out in the world again just yet.'

'You are so kind,' said Norman.

'I'm not kind. It's just sensible, that's all.'

It *was* kind. But he did not want to be Jonquil's possession, Jonquil's pet. As the weeks passed, he found himself acting as her escort when she went out in the evenings, and when she entertained at home. He knew that many men would have given anything for a life of such ease and privilege. But, if he were not strong enough now, when would he ever be? He began to apply for jobs secretly as they were advertised in the pages of the newspapers.

He did not know whether she noticed that he had started to get more post than usual, but his applications did not lead to employment. Computer programmers needed special training, apparently; so did policemen. He was not even interviewed by Oxfam or Help The Aged, who needed Charity Organizers. Perhaps it was not, after all, what he was cut out to be. He wondered if there would be any point in giving the Church of England another try. He knew, roughly speaking, what was required of a parson; and it was the only profession, apart from Parliament and the Ballet, where the word stamped so ignominiously on his passport would seem a positive recommendation. But the thought of the church exhausted him. It seemed all very well at first, and then it had a way of going wrong.

As he read more and more mystics, Norman wondered why that should be. In many ways, religion was so obviously an admirable and necessary thing. And yet, it never seemed to make anyone any better. The reverse was more often the case.

When he discussed the problem of what to do with Mungo Dundee, his friend seemed as if he was going to be of no more use than Jonquil.

'Why have a job at all?' he asked in a wounded tone of voice. He had never taken employment of any kind. He thought of it as something which people only did who did not have the imagination to do anything more interesting – visiting relations, for example, or studying architecture.

They were ambling down Jermyn Street, where Mungo had ordered half a dozen shirts.

'I need the money,' said Norman.

'Can't you get money without having a job? Sell some shares or something?'

'And I really ought to be independent of Jonquil. She's rather taken me over since Lubbock died.'

'One had noticed. But in many ways, that is very nice. I can't make up my mind whether I would like it or not. I like her house, except that the staircase is in the wrong place.'

'My father thought I was going back into teaching.'

'You rather enjoyed that, didn't you? Where was it? Haileybury?'

'No, Peacham House.'

'It seems the obvious solution, if you really enjoyed it. I wonder why you think there's a problem.'

It did seem the obvious solution. The conversation with Mungo cleared the air. Once more, after such a long period of stagnation and inertia, he saw the way forward.

There was an educational agency not two hundred yards from where they were standing, and Mungo took him there at once. They hurtled up two floors in an old-fashioned cage-lift and emerged into offices which retained about them the peculiar atmosphere of English private schools. The secretaries did not look like office-workers at all. They all looked as if they had just come in from shrieking their heads off on the touchline. And men in tweed coats and crumpled flannel trousers flitted about smoking pipes, whether officials of the agency or the ghosts of preparatory school masters, swathed in a mist of cheap tobacco-smoke, who could say?

Norman filled in a form while Mungo watched. He stated his age, his teaching experience, and the subjects that he was prepared to teach.

'Just English and History?' asked one of the spectral schoolmasters. 'That won't get you very far, I'm afraid, at this time of year. We've got a vacancy here for a chaplaincy in the West Riding. How about that?'

'No thanks.'

'Well, say you can teach French and German, and a bit of Science, and we'll keep you posted.'

True to their word, particulars of jobs came rolling in by almost every post. At first, Norman wondered whether they had taken any notice of the information he had provided. He kept receiving details of Geography posts in Northern Ireland or Gymnastics in Great Malvern. There *was* an interesting looking job at an English school in Switzerland, but when he wrote to find out about it, he received a letter back saying that the post had already been filled. The beginning of the new school year was hard upon him, and he began to give up hope, when, one day at breakfast, light dawned.

'What's that, dear?' Jonquil asked, as she pierced her yoghourt carton with a teaspoon.

'Oh, nothing.'

'I wonder if you could help entertain Father Sporran at luncheon today. He's bringing over a manuscript for me to look at. It's going to be called *The New Tomorrow*. Rather a good title, I think . . .'

Her voice lilted on, in its poetic way, while Norman read the particulars. It wasn't very much money, and the school was not even I.A.P.S. They wanted a bachelor – not of Arts, simply a bachelor – to teach General Subjects to eighty boys between the ages of eight and thirteen, in preparation for the Common Entrance Examination. Norman wondered what General Subjects were, but he supposed that he would easily find out. The school was in Cornwall, too, which sounded pleasant.

'Shotty, dear, I don't believe you've been listening. I said that some of the sisters are coming.'

He finished writing his *curriculum vitae* in his bedroom, and realized that he had taken all morning over it. Out of the window, he could see nuns dancing on the lawn.

Mother Teresa had written a new song and its haunting tones drifted up to him on the warm September breeze.

'Join the dance of love!
Come and follow me!
Let the Holy Spirit
Make you free, free, free!'

He wondered if he would ever be rid of these women in their gym-slips, who scampered and pirouetted across his horizon so often, like Norns or Furies. He felt in no mood to join any dance, still less a dance of love. There were too many pitfalls, and too many ways of going wrong. He knew now that Liz would never have made him happy. He was doomed

184

to be solitary, like his father, wandering from place to place on the earth, a stranger and a sojourner. With one half of himself, he longed for dullness and safety and security. With another half of himself, he wanted even more the illusion of freedom, at whatever risk.

'Free! Free!
Let the Holy Spirit
Make you free, free, free!'

He had learnt quite enough of the world since living with Jonquil to know that the notion of human freedom was a totally artificial one which we try to impose on our existence in order to give ourselves dignity. But, however obvious it was, he rebelled against the idea. He was her prisoner here, and unless he made some decisive move soon, it would be too late. With an iron will, he finished writing NEAR POLPERRO on the envelope and slipped out to the post.

11

THOSE ANGEL FACES SMILE

His spirits were high as he changed trains at Truro. Jonquil had been much more reasonable than he feared she would be. Father Sporran had persuaded her that it would be a good thing if Norman had a life of his own; and, as he himself had said, there were always the holidays. She had dabbed the corner of her eyes a little, but she said that Shotty had always known that she had no wish to stand in the way of his career. And Cornwall was such a magical place – so many saints, and spirits, and strange atmospheres.

The magic took a little time to sink in. The landscape was

unwelcoming and bleak, and it was the end of the holiday season. At every town they stopped at, it smelt as if they had sprayed the streets with hot fat and vinegar, while in the distance caravans and chalets sprawled in unending lines over the blighted landscape. Every dustbin would be full, and every hedgerow chock-a-block with ice-cream papers and used contraceptives.

The school was in a remote little village which could only be reached by bus. Although it was very near the coast, the dirty sea was invisible because of the way the dark land sloped up towards it. Norman saw only a few ugly little pink-washed houses huddling near an over-restored church and then a lane which wandered round into muddy nothingness.

'Tregorran Hall?'

The lady in the Post Office seemed astonished that anyone should be asking for it.

'There be no school there.'

'But I had a letter from there only the other day.'

'That's as may be. Tregorran Hall has stood empty this many a long year. Ever since her ladyship was *took*.'

'*Took*?'

'Ar. Folks hereabouts don't go near the Hall. Some says there's hobgoblins, and such.'

'All the same, I should like you to direct me to it.'

The lady gave him some unhelpful suggestions and smirked maliciously when the little bell on the door rang and Norman had left the shop. She did not like folk from London and always did her best to scare them.

It worried Norman. He did not believe in hobgoblins, but Jonquil had been sure that anywhere in Cornwall would bring him in touch with the supernatural. And it seemed vaguely sinister that even the Post Office should not have heard of the school.

The Hall lay a little way out of the village. There was nothing to indicate that it was a school. TREGORRAN HALL, in very faded lettering, was engraved on the stone gateposts, under which someone had stuck a notice which read FRESH

He wondered what oodles were; or whether it was a mis-spelling for BREAD, and whether oodles bread was a Cornish delicacy. He imagined it as rather soft, doughy stuff. But a yapping sound in the courtyard indicated his mistake. There seemed to be dozens of woolly dogs milling round a stoutly built middle-aged woman in gum-boots. Almost a flock of them.

'About time, too,' she said. 'We were expecting you at nine o'clock this morning.'

'I'm sorry. I understood I was expected at four o'clock.'

'Don't palm me off with that twaddle. You were expected at nine. Now, get on with it, and don't expect any tea until you've finished.'

The mention of tea awakened a longing in the taste-buds which, in his anxiety, Norman had almost forgotten.

'Get on with what?'

'De-lousing the little beasts. You heard what I told you on the telephone.'

'I think there must be some mistake,' said Norman. 'I've come about the teaching job.'

'The what?'

'The teaching job.'

'So you aren't the vet?'

'No.'

'Well, why didn't you say so? I hope you can cook. I'm Mrs Ritchie-Bannister, the headmaster's sister. Don't take any notice of what he says. I hope you like dogs.'

'Moderately.'

'Twaddle. You either like them or you don't like them.'

'I like them.'

'Then why didn't you say so? That's the school, as you can see.'

She indicated an epidemic of jerry-built excrescences which were ruining the side of a rather stately old house. Beyond it, there were some Nissen-huts, evidently being used as class-rooms.

'Have you just been in prison?' she asked, as they walked

towards the house.

'No.'

'What they call hospital?'

'I was in hospital not long ago as a matter of fact.'

'I thought so. We only get criminals and loonies applying. You don't mind my calling them loonies?'

'No, but I was in a hospital . . .'

'Of course you were. But I believe in calling a spade a spade. You'll find my brother in there,' she said, when they reached the front door. 'Don't listen to anything he says about the dogs.'

'I won't.'

'I expect I'll be able to find you some tea when you've finished with him.'

In the hall, Norman met a crumpled little man with a yellow face and a cigarette hanging out of his mouth.

'Muldoon,' he said.

'No, Shotover.'

'Really? I was sure I was called Muldoon. But you may be right. Come in anyway, my dear fellow. You must have come about the job.'

He led Norman into a large room full of obsolescent office-furniture. There was a calendar on the wall for 1947. Everything was swathed in thick cigarette-smoke, and on every available surface there were ash-trays overflowing with stubs.

'You don't mind if I smoke?'

'Not at all.'

'People say it's bad for you, but it never seems to have done me any harm.'

He coughed weakly. Norman thought that he might drop dead at any minute. The thought even crossed his mind, as they sat looking at each other silently, that the little man might already be dead.

'Now,' said Mr Muldoon. 'The job.'

'Yes,' said Norman. 'What exactly does it entail?'

'Well, general subjects, as I say. You didn't speak to my sister on the way in, did you?'

'Yes.'

'Don't take any notice of what she says. I hope you don't like poodles?'

'Not really.'

'Nor do I. They are so *upsetting*. Now, I see that you are a bachelor.'

'Yes.'

'Good, good. I find that married men are so unreliable. Ambitious, if you know what I mean.'

'Yes.'

'You aren't ambitious?'

'Not in the least.'

'Then I'll take you to see my little *pupils*.'

He laughed airily.

'Term can't have started already,' said Norman.

'But they have nowhere to go to, poor pets.'

'No mothers or fathers?'

'Some of them have mothers and fathers, but they usually stay with us.'

'Really?'

'Come and see my *class-rooms*.'

Mr Muldoon sniggered again and lit another cigarette before pottering out into the hall again. He led the way down a long corridor, opened two or three green baize doors, and sidled out into a playground.

'How did you hear about me?' he asked as they walked along.

'Through the agency.'

'What agency?'

Norman named it.

This seemed to amuse Mr Muldoon very much.

'I'm still on their lists?' he asked. He coughed again and swayed to and fro on his heels in quiet amusement. 'I always left particulars with them in the old days,' he said. 'I put *general subjects* because one never knew when a vacancy was going to occur. But it's a long time since we had any er – *staff*. You'll have the whole common-room to yourself.'

'Really?'

'Yes, really.'

'You mean I shall be teaching eighty or so boys all on my own?'

'Ah,' said Mr Muldoon. '*Boys*. They were such a trouble. Always misbehaving themselves and having to be given the cane. And the parents took up so much time. They seemed to demand *everything*, and, really, the fees were quite moderate. If they had wanted laboratories and swimming-pools, they should have sent their sons somewhere else. I drew the line at a gymnasium. As you probably know, by definition a gymnasium is a place where people sport themselves in the *altogether*.'

'Is it?'

'Oh yes. Greek *gumnas*, naked, you know.'

'Of course.'

'With the type of man we had teaching here in those days, it would have been very unsuitable.'

'Yes.'

'Boys were a bother,' he said. 'We were always having the police round. My present little *academy* is much more to my taste.'

He flung open the door of a Nissen-hut. About eight chimpanzees in blazers, shorts, grey flannel shirts and striped ties rose to their feet politely and sniggered. Mr Muldoon sniggered back.

'You can sit down now,' he told them. 'This is your new master, Mr . . . Mr, what was it?'

'Shotover. But I really think, in the circumstances that I ought not . . . '

'Ought not to what, my dear fellow?'

'Stay.'

'Come, come, Mr Shotover. I never heard of anything so ridiculous. Half an hour of Greek verbs with these little chaps, and then change their trousers. It smells as if they'll need it. My sister usually makes some tea at about five o'clock, but take no notice.'

'I was under the impression . . . I certainly don't want to stay.'

190

The chimpanzees grinned at him and scratched their armpits.

'You really have very little choice, do you, Mr Shotover? We can't let you go, I'm afraid. It's against the school rules.'

'I insist that you let me go.'

But Mr Muldoon had already left the classroom, and Norman heard the click as he locked the door. He looked at the windows, but they were the sort which only opened at the top and which were impossible to climb through. The row of happy little faces looked up at him imploringly. He walked to the desk and sat down.

'Perhaps,' he said, 'instead of Greek verbs, this afternoon we will start to read *Macbeth*.'

BESTSELLING FICTION FROM ARROW

All these books are available from your bookshop or news-agent or you can order them direct. Just tick the titles you want and complete the form below.

THE DEFECTOR	Evelyn Anthony	£1.75
THE HISTORY MAN	Malcolm Bradbury	£1.75
1985	Anthony Burgess	£1.75
THE BILLION DOLLAR KILLING	Paul Erdman	£1.75
THE YEAR OF THE FRENCH	Thomas Flanagan	£2.50
EMMA SPARROW	Marie Joseph	£1.60
COCKPIT	Jerzy Kosinski	£1.60
CITY OF THE DEAD	Herbert Lieberman	£1.60
STRUMPET CITY	James Plunkett	£2.50
TO GLORY WE STEER	Alexander Kent	£1.75
TORPEDO RUN	Douglas Reeman	£1.50
THE BEST MAN TO DIE	Ruth Rendell	£1.25
SCENT OF FEAR	Margaret Yorke	£1.25
2001: A SPACE ODYSSEY	Arthur C. Clarke	£1.50
THE RUNNING YEARS	Claire Rayner	£2.50
	Postage	_____
	Total	_____

ARROW BOOKS, BOOKSERVICE BY POST, PO BOX 29, DOUGLAS, ISLE OF MAN, BRITISH ISLES

Please enclose a cheque or postal order made out to Arrow Books Limited for the amount due including 10p per book for postage and packing for orders within the UK and 12p for overseas orders.

Please print clearly

NAME ....

ADDRESS ....

....

Whilst every effort is made to keep prices down and to keep popular books in print, Arrow Books cannot guarantee that prices will be the same as those advertised here or that the books will be available.